Dear Romance Reader,

Welcome to a world of breathtaking passion and never-ending romance.

Welcome to *Precious Gem Romances*.

It is our pleasure to present *Precious Gem Romances,* a wonderful new line of romance books by some of America's best-loved authors. Let these thrilling historical and contemporary romances sweep you away to far-off times and places in stories that will dazzle your senses and melt your heart.

Sparkling with joy, laughter, and love, each *Precious Gem Romance* glows with all the passion and excitement you expect from the very best in romance. Offered at a great affordable price, these books are an irresistible value—and an essential addition to your romance collection. Tender love stories you will want to read again and again, *Precious Gem Romances* are books you will treasure forever.

Look for eight fabulous new *Precious Gem Romances* each month—available only at Wal★Mart.

Lynn Brown, Publisher

# TOUCH OF TEXAS

## Judy Christenberry

Zebra Books
Kensington Publishing Corp.

ZEBRA BOOKS are published by

Kensington Publishing Corp.
850 Third Avenue
New York, NY 10022

First Printing: October, 1996
10  9  8  7  6  5  4  3  2  1

Printed in the United States of America

# Chapter One

Damn.

God must not've been listening.

He'd prayed for an uptight, homely spinster. No such luck. He didn't need this kind of temptation now that he'd decided what he had to do.

The man beside him whistled under his breath. "You think that's her?"

"Nobody else got out of the plane," Matt Griffin muttered as he settled his cowboy hat more firmly on his head. "Come on. Let's go welcome her to town."

"But do you think she'll even consider us? I mean, look at her. Gosh darn it, she's pretty enough to be a movie star."

"You just remember what I said, Samuel," Matt warned. "There's to be no matchmaking. Period. None. I'm not part of the package deal." Not that he wouldn't enjoy socializing with the beautiful doctor. But a sophisticated, career woman wasn't what he was looking for. He'd already married one of those. And she'd left him. Now he was going to marry a homebody, someone who would have his kids and make family her career.

"Aw, Matt, you know we were just joshin'," Sam Dryson replied.

"Just remember. Besides, it's not her beauty that makes me wonder if she'll consider us. She was one of the top graduates in her class, and her recommendations were the best. What's she doing in Griffin?"

Sam didn't attempt to respond to Matt's question. He couldn't, Matt knew. Only the doctor could supply that answer.

He strode across the tarmac, the sheriff by his side, his eyes never leaving the sophisticated beauty beside the plane. She was dressed in designer clothes, high heels, and with an expensive watch on her wrist. Not the norm for an isolated west Texas town. He'd worked hard for this moment, for his town, the people in it. He hoped she wasn't a mirage.

Standing at the bottom of the steps from the plane, she was talking with the pilot, Preston Lewis, an old friend of Matt's, as if she were in a fashionable bar. Instead, she was standing on a deserted runway, the sun beating down on her and dust blowing around her skirt.

Her short skirt. Revealing very shapely legs. Double damn.

"Mornin', Preston," Matt said with a nod before turning to the woman beside his friend. "Ma'am." He touched the brim of his hat. "Are you Dr. Kelly?"

Her full lips parted to reveal perfect teeth. The smile, while charming, seemed a shade hesitant to Matt. She couldn't be nervous about the interview. Even if she'd been only an average student, which she wasn't, the town fathers would welcome her as if she were Einstein.

And she couldn't be worried about how any male would respond to her either. Matt felt his temperature rise just looking at her.

"Yes, I'm Susan Kelly." She extended her hand just like the man he wished she was. He wrapped his hard, callused fingers around her soft skin and barely repressed a shiver.

"I'm Matt Griffin, the mayor of Griffin." He lost himself staring into her blue eyes, framed by lush, dark lashes, not releasing her hand until Sam nudged him. "This is Samuel Dryson, sheriff hereabouts."

The grizzled sheriff beamed at her, already entranced. And Matt couldn't blame him. Her beauty made it easy to forget the reason she was here.

"Welcome, Dr. Kelly. We're sure happy to have you visit us." He took off his Stetson and held it in his hands, grinning at her.

There was an awkward silence that increased Matt's uneasiness. She didn't look any more comfortable than his ex-wife had when she first arrived in Griffin. He'd tried to warn Lindsay of its isolation, before she married him, but she'd insisted she would love his hometown. He hoped the doctor would adjust better than Lindsay had, or all their hard work would be wasted.

"Preston, if you'll get Dr. Kelly's bags, we'll take her on into town."

The pilot hauled four large suitcases, in matching leather, from the back of the airplane, causing both waiting men to stare. Matt almost groaned aloud. Another clotheshorse, like Lindsay. No one should need four bags for a three-day stay. After saying goodbye to Preston, Matt picked up two bags and the sheriff claimed the others.

"This way, ma'am," Matt added, gesturing toward the side of the air field where he'd parked. He watched her struggle through the baked grass and dirt in high heels, a rueful grin on his face. She'd probably thought there'd be an airport, with paved walks.

At least her hair-do was practical. Her dark hair was plaited in a French braid. Matt couldn't help wondering what it would look like unbound, flowing over her slender shoulders. He looked away before he could be caught staring.

"We're sure glad you're interested in moving to Griffin," Sam said as he trudged alongside her. "Wait 'til you see the pretty little hospital we built."

"Yes, I'm looking forward to it," she murmured, her voice low and musical, drawing Matt's gaze again. She was as delicate as a hothouse orchid. What in the hell was she doing out here in the middle of nowhere?

"Where—where is the town?" she asked after a moment, her gaze darting around her.

"It's about five miles thattaway," Sam assured her. "You'll like it. We're real friendly. Lots of nice people. We even have a movie house that gets movies only a couple of months after Dallas."

"How nice," she said faintly, her eyes wide.

Matt stared at her. Something was wrong here. This woman wasn't acting like an enthusiastic visitor. He'd been surprised when she'd responded to their request for an interview, and he still didn't understand why, with her qualifications, she was here. As scarce as doctors were, especially those willing to forego the money opportunities in the big cities, he'd been surprised they'd received any response at all.

"And, no matter what you hear, we don't get that many dust storms," Sam added.

Almost groaning aloud, Matt decided he'd made a mistake inviting the sheriff to accompany him. At this rate, they wouldn't even get Dr. Kelly to his jeep before she ran for the plane.

"Dust storms?" Those incredible blue eyes were again wide, with apprehension, he thought, and he hastened to reassure her.

"Sam's just teasing. We do have an occasional dust storm, but they're not that bad. On the other hand, we have a lot of beautiful days like today." And it was beautiful. The sky was a bright blue with no clouds, and the air, while heavy with heat, was crystal clear.

"It's rather hot," she murmured.

"True," Matt agreed, "but I'm sure it's hot in Dallas, too, in the summer. At least our heat is dry, which makes it not seem quite so bad. And we do have air conditioning in Griffin."

"Yes, of course." She still sounded unenthusiastic to Matt's ear.

They reached the Jeep Cherokee, its red paint dimmed with a thin layer of dust, and stowed her bags in the back. Opening the passenger door for her, Matt waited until she was seated, admiring her long legs in the process, and then closed the door. Once he was behind the wheel, he asked the question that was bothering him. "Just why are you interested in moving to Griffin?"

Dead silence greeted his question. Finally, she said, "I specialized in family medicine."

"Yes, ma'am," Sam agreed enthusiastically from the back seat. "That's what Matt said we needed. We're tickled pink that you chose us."

The flush that filled her porcelain cheeks made Matt uneasy. He hurried to reassure her. "We realize this is just a visit, not a commitment, Dr. Kelly. Sam got a little carried away."

"Yes, just a visit. I'm visiting several communities to—to decide where I'll set up my practice."

"Griffin's a pretty little town. I know you'll like it," Samuel assured her again.

Matt said nothing.

Everyone remained silent until they entered the small town, a mixture of old frame buildings and a few modern, adobe structures, two-pump filling stations and one modern twelve-pump, self-serve oasis, a meshing of old and new.

"Is there a hotel?" Dr. Kelly asked, shifting in her seat, her gaze darting from one side of the main street to the other.

"There's a motel, but we thought you might prefer Georgy's," Matt explained.

"Who is Georgy?"

"She's Matt's aunt," Sam explained.

Matt caught the quick glance that landed on him before she turned away. The woman was unusually nervous. The foreboding that had been growing in him only got worse. Had they worked so hard for nothing? Was their only chance for a doctor going to be lost before they could even try to impress their visitor?

He stopped his jeep in front of an elegant Victorian house, its yard neatly trimmed and unusually green, its walls blindingly white.

"How charming!" The doctor's reaction was the first one of approval she'd shown. The smile on her lips was genuine and damn sexy, Matt decided. He looked away.

The sheriff agreed. "Yep. Georgy has a nice place."

Matt got out and came around to open her door and help her out of his jeep. The reaction he'd felt earlier when he'd taken her hand greeted him again as he touched her. This lady was going to complicate his life if she stayed.

As Susan slid down from the high seat, she noticed several people standing on the sidewalk nearby. Where had they come from? They smiled widely and nodded their heads.

She nodded back, not sure whom she was greeting.

The sheriff, having gotten out also, waved a hand in the townspeople's direction. "Come on, now, folks, give the doc some breathing room. You'll meet her at the reception."

The sheriff took her arm and escorted her past the white picket gate that swung open easily, up the sidewalk to the front door. The brass knocker shone from a recent polish, and he rapped smartly on it.

The door was instantly swung open by a middle-aged woman of Mexican descent.

"Hi, Maria. Where's Georgy?"

"I'm right here, Sam," a cool, pleasing voice responded.

Susan turned to discover her hostess, still a beauty in her early fifties, dressed in a silk dress every bit as fashionable as any seen in Dallas.

"Aw, Georgy, don't you look fine. This here is the doc. Doc, Georgy Griffin."

"Miss Griffin, I'm delighted to meet you." Susan extended a hand, suddenly feeling more sure of herself. She'd been trained from an early age in social expertise. Greeting a lady

in a parlor was different from the meeting with the two men at
the airstrip. Especially the handsome cowboy with his difficult
questions.

"Welcome to Griffin, Doctor." The charming smile that
accompanied her words set Susan at ease.

She accepted Georgy's unspoken invitation to sit down in
the comfortable parlor before asking the question that was
causing her heart to pound. "The sheriff mentioned a reception?" She hoped her voice was casual.

Georgy sent a look of exasperation toward the other two.
"Didn't they explain? Men! They were supposed to fill you in
on all the events scheduled. If you don't think you can manage
everything, just let me know. We've planned a town-wide
reception this evening. Sort of a pot luck dinner. Everyone's
so anxious to meet you."

"I'm looking forward to meeting them, too." She intended
to sound sincere. In fact, she really did want to meet the townspeople. But she had more pressing needs. A lift of one eyebrow
from the mayor told her she hadn't convinced him.

She'd been shocked at his appearance. In his letters, he'd
sounded like he'd lived in Griffin at least a hundred years. Not
only was he only a few years older than her, probably in his
early thirties, but he also appeared educated, intelligent and as
handsome as any man she'd ever seen. His lion-eyed gaze
seemed to go right through her, however, and she didn't want
her secrets revealed. Not yet, anyway.

"Will everyone be there?" she asked. The mayor's gaze
grew even more intent and she hurriedly added with a shaky
laugh, "I don't even know exactly how many people that will
be."

Georgy patted her arm with soft fingers. "And no reason
you should know, dear. We're larger than we look, actually.
There are almost five thousand people around here. Not all of
them live in the town proper, but they'd be your patients."

"I see."

"If you decide to move here," Matt added. She looked away

from his penetrating gaze and caught the surprised look his aunt sent him.

"Have they told you about the medical center we've built?" Georgy asked, as if to distract her from her nephew.

"I believe Mayor Griffin mentioned it in his letters." She could scarcely remember the details of his letters. Her interest, apprehension even, had been centered on something else.

"It's not big, you know, just six beds, but sufficient. And we decorated it nicely," Georgy added. "I was in charge of the decorations."

"I'm sure it's lovely."

"We wouldn't have managed it without Matt," the sheriff added. "He was tireless workin' for it, even during calving season. He bullied just about everyone into helping."

The younger man actually looked embarrassed at the praise, making him all the more attractive. There was strength in his features that Susan found appealing. And yet, his blond good looks, reminding her of her ex-husband, made her uneasy.

"We all worked on it, Sam, not just me. This town pulls together," Matt said, his gaze having returned to her. "Everyone has worked very hard to have a doctor here."

He seemed to be making a point, but Susan was too anxious to pay attention. The closer she got to the moment she'd been waiting for, the more distracted she was. And the mayor's sharp-eyed gaze and sexy good looks didn't help. With what she hoped was a gracious smile, she asked, "Would it be possible for me to go to my room? I'm afraid the flight tired me out. I'd like to rest before the reception this evening."

"Why, of course, honey. I'll get Rico to take up your bags. He's Maria's husband. The two of them take care of me." Georgy said.

"I'd better help him," Matt said, standing. Susan had no difficulty reading the man's mind this time. After all, it was only a repeat of his reaction when he'd first seen her four bags. She knew she'd packed too much, but she'd been so undecided about what she should bring, she'd finally given up and brought it all.

"I'm afraid I overpacked a little. I wasn't sure what would be appropriate." She directed her apology to the sheriff and Georgy rather than the mayor.

"Has my nephew been teasing you about that? He always complains about the same thing with me. Just ignore him. He needs to use those muscles for something, anyway." Georgy chuckled and Susan couldn't help but join in. Her gaze drifted over the tall man frowning at his aunt. He certainly had enough muscle to manage more luggage than she owned.

"I didn't complain at all," he protested to Georgy, but he avoided looking at Susan.

"I should hope not. Ladies need more gear than men. But then, we look better, too." Georgy patted her hair in imitation of a femme fatale and everyone laughed again.

Matt's lion eyes turned to Susan, and she was annoyed by the rising tension she felt as she responded to his appraisal. A small frown formed before she could erase it. She wasn't interested in the mayor, no matter how handsome he was. She wasn't interested in any man . . . in *that* way. And she'd better keep reminding herself of that, she decided as she looked away.

Without another word, Matt left the room. Georgy stared after him speculatively and then turned to Susan. "I think you've impressed my nephew. 'Course, I'm not surprised, you're such a pretty little thing."

"I don't think 'little' is quite how to describe me, Miss Griffin. I'm five-eight."

"Call me Georgy, child. We're not formal out here. And next to Matt, you'd be considered little." She leaned forward, as if confiding a secret, and added, "He's not married, you know."

Susan answered the woman's revelation with a small smile, her eyes wide, but she could think of nothing to say. She refused to acknowledge the flicker of interest in her heart.

"Now, Georgy," the sheriff intervened, "Matt warned us both not to—"

"Not to what?" the subject of their discussion asked as he entered the room. He stood there, his hands on his trim hips, waiting for an answer.

Even Georgy seemed intimidated by her nephew's attitude. "Why, I don't see what the problem is," she huffed, turning toward Susan rather than her nephew.

"Georgy?" he prompted, not put off by her fussing.

"I was just filling in Susan—I can call you Susan, can't I?" Georgy asked, and Susan knew she was stalling.

She tried to assist her. "Of course you may. Georgy just explained that everyone is informal out here."

"I don't think that's what she wasn't supposed to tell you, Doctor," the determined man said and then turned back to his aunt. "Well, Georgy?"

"For heaven's sake, Matthew, I just told Susan that you weren't married. There's nothing wrong with that." In spite of her words, Georgy's red cheeks proclaimed she'd been caught doing something she knew she wasn't supposed to do.

"I doubt that information is of any interest to Dr. Kelly. She's here to look at setting up a medical practice, not to play Griffin's version of the dating game." He turned to Susan and she sank her teeth into her bottom lip. "Just ignore my aunt. I'll be here at six-thirty to take you and Georgy to the reception."

"Thank you." What else could she say? She supposed she could reassure him that she wasn't looking for a husband, but she doubted that he'd believe her. Matt Griffin was probably the town's most eligible bachelor. Somehow, she suspected he'd been pursued by every woman in town at one time or another.

"Ready to go, Sam?" Matt prodded the older man who'd said nothing since he'd reentered the room.

"Right, Matt. See you this evening, Doc. It was a pleasure meetin' you. I'm sure you're gonna like it here in Griffin."

"Thank you, Sheriff," Susan murmured. She stood and

extended her hand to him, and he took it with a smile. Then, out of courtesy, she had to shake Matt Griffin's hand also. His warm fingers wrapped around hers and she pulled away as soon as possible. The man's touch shouldn't affect her as it did.

He stared down at her, as if trying to read something in her eyes, and she looked away. Feeling the heat in her cheeks, she prayed he'd leave without commenting on her behavior. Maybe she really was tired.

She must be. Because, just for a moment, she'd even forgotten her real purpose in coming to Griffin, Texas.

# Chapter Two

Would he recognize her?

Susan studied her features in the mirror. Her grandmother had always said she looked like her mother, and she hadn't been able to remember enough of her father to know differently. But the picture she'd found tucked away in her mother's lingerie drawer after her death told her there were traces of her father in her features.

Her face was stronger than her mother's. Poor Mother. She'd always suffered from ill health. It was her mother's pain that had first led her to an interest in medicine. Susan would've done anything to alleviate her mother's suffering. Grandmother had protested Susan's decision. Not ladylike, she'd said, pressing her lips tightly together.

That was the greatest of all sins. Not being a lady.

Grandmother had considered her father's greatest sin that of not being a gentleman, her interpretation of wealth and social prestige. Until six months ago, Susan had thought his greatest sin had been leaving.

Now she knew differently.

But she was afraid her knowledge came too late. He might never forgive her. That was one of the reasons why she'd come to Griffin without contacting him. She wanted him to get to know her before he—he rejected her as he'd been rejected.

She was ashamed to admit the other reason. Her grandmother had always told her her father left because he couldn't touch her mother's money. She'd told Susan his only interest in his child had been the hope of getting control of her money. Though Susan didn't want to believe those cold words, she was being cautious.

Now that she was alone, she longed for family, for someone who cared. Her one attempt to build her own family had been a disaster, resulting in divorce. Her ex-husband, like her grandmother, had wanted her as a satellite, not a person in her own right. Too late, she'd also discovered his interest in her finances.

"Susan? Are you ready? Matt's down below waiting for us," Georgy called through the door.

Susan drew a deep breath, lifted her chin and tried to ignore the extra shivers of excitement brought on by the man downstairs. She needed to concentrate on the evening before her. If she wanted this chance to know her father, she had to convince the townspeople to accept her as their doctor. Was her blue coat dress okay? Should she have left her hair in its french braid?

"Susan?"

"I'm coming, Georgy." Too late now to change her appearance. She hurried to the door.

"Oh, my, child, don't you look pretty! Doesn't she, Matt?" Georgy called down the stairs as she pulled Susan after her.

"Dr. Kelly looks most attractive," Matt agreed solemnly.

Susan could've said the same thing about him. The man was wearing a tan sports coat over an open-necked yellow shirt and pressed jeans. His golden lion-eyes, tawny blond hair and deep tan gave him a surfer look that was belied by his muscular build.

Trying to control the heat she felt rising in her cheeks, she greeted him coolly. "Good evening, Mayor."

"Now, you two mustn't be so formal. Everyone will think you don't like each other, and we can't have that." Georgy looked at each of them expectantly.

Matt gave a sigh that was a protest in itself, and Susan felt a nudge of irritation. While she wasn't entranced with her looks, she'd been told often enough by men that she was attractive. But the mayor acted as if being friendly was a penance. Which was doubly hard to accept when she reacted so strongly every time she got near him.

Raising her eyebrows in challenge, she murmured, "No, we wouldn't want them to think that, would we, Matt?"

"Of course not, Susan." He stared up the stairs at her, and she almost missed a step. The man had sex appeal just oozing out of him. Why wasn't he married? Surely there were a few single women out here in this desert.

"Shall we go?" he prompted, awakening Susan from her thoughts. She continued down the stairs after Georgy.

"Of course. I'm anxious to meet everyone."

When she saw Matt's gaze narrow, she was afraid she'd given herself away. Between this man's sexual vitality that left her spinning and the anticipation of seeing her father, she could barely maintain her composure.

Though the cafe where they were having the reception was only four blocks away, Matt drove them in his Jeep Cherokee with the air conditioning going full blast. The sun was on the horizon, but its heat was still powerful.

She was unaware she was chewing on her bottom lip until Georgy leaned forward from the back seat to pat her shoulder. "Don't you be nervous, now, Susan. Everyone is going to love you. Why, I reckon you may even get a marriage proposal or two out of some lovesick cowpoke. Ladies like you don't come along every day."

"Thank you, Georgy, but I'm not interested in—in marriage. Establishing a practice will talk all my energies, I imagine."

She didn't let her gaze wander to the driver to see his reaction, but she felt him stiffen beside her.

She slipped from the jeep without his assistance, not anxious to have him touch her. Already tense with the ordeal before her, she didn't need the additional stimulation his closeness brought. Just a chemical reaction, she decided, like caffeine or something.

"This way . . . Susan. The town awaits you."

There was a hint of sarcasm that drew a quick glance before she preceded him into the cafe. She wondered how big a vote the mayor had in the decision to offer her a contract.

The crowd already gathered surged forward as she entered and, to her surprise, Matt stepped in front of her and ran interference, reaching behind him for her hand to pull her along. The warmth of his touch gave her an unexpected surge of strength. Once he reached the far side of the large room, he turned and spoke.

"Let's not overwhelm Dr. Kelly. Form a reception line and you can each come by and greet her and then serve yourselves some of the good homecooking we've got here tonight."

With Georgy on one side of her and Matt on the other, Susan began shaking hands with the people of Griffin. Even as she smiled and made small talk, she scanned the crowd for a man she hadn't seen since she was three years old. Her father.


Matt introduced his neighbors and friends to the doctor almost automatically. His mind was occupied with her reaction rather than his actions.

Something about her bothered him.

He almost chuckled aloud to himself. That was an understatement, but he wasn't thinking about his physical response to the beautiful woman beside him. That was probably a given for most of the men in the room. She was a beauty, no doubt about it.

Was it her uneasiness with a small town in the middle of

nowhere? Her citified ways? He couldn't condemn someone right off the bat just because she packed a lot of clothes or wore inappropriate shoes. If carrying four bags was the price to pay for the way she looked tonight, he'd probably offer to be a permanent bellboy for her.

Her perfume alone would justify a lot of luggage. He leaned a little closer and unobtrusively sniffed the air, his lungs filling with a light floral aroma with just a hint of mystery. That scent would haunt him for days if he wasn't careful.

And her hair. The dark silken curtain that hung almost to her waist begged to be stroked, touched. His body tightened as he imagined running his fingers through its shining length.

"Matt? You forgotten my name?" one of his old neighbors asked, staring at him in surprise.

"Of course not, Odie." He introduced the man and his wife, reminding himself to concentrate on the present. If not, he was going to embarrass himself in several ways.

The man behind Odie, gray-haired and tall, turned around to answer a question just before he reached Matt and Susan. Focusing his attention on his duties, Matt suddenly realized Susan had stiffened. He looked down at her to discover her intent gaze on the gray-haired man.

"Something wrong?" he whispered even as Jinks Maloney turned back to greet them.

Unable to wait for an answer to his question, Matt introduced the older man and almost felt the sigh that Susan quietly released.

And that was what bothered him about Dr. Susan Kelly. He couldn't explain it, but he thought the doctor had a different agenda than he'd expected. He wasn't sure she was here to actually consider their town as her future headquarters.

If that wasn't her reason for coming, what was? And how could she do such damage to a town which had struggled and worked hard to find a doctor?

Since he could find no answers to his questions, Matt concentrated on the woman beside him. Alerted to her tension, Matt watched her stiffen each time an older man was introduced. She relaxed again once Matt said the name. It was unnerving, kind of like playing Russian Roulette, wondering if the next name would bring about whatever reaction was waiting in the wings.

What was she doing? Who was she looking for? Because that had to be the cause of her stress. She was expecting to meet someone here. Who? And for what reason?

Numerous reasons for her tension suggested themselves, but Matt didn't like any of them. He particularly dismissed the idea of Susan Kelly having had an affair with someone in Griffin. He was sure she was too young and too far away for that explanation. Of course, it was none of his business unless it affected her decision about Griffin.

His only concern was the town's future.

*Yeah, right.*

"Could I have a glass of water?" Susan whispered.

"I'll get it for you, dear," Georgy whispered in return, leaving Susan and Matt to face the line still wending its way past the visiting doctor.

"Are you all right?" he asked, lowering his head to look at her. Her porcelain features seemed even paler than ever. Her skin would toughen if she stayed in Griffin, he speculated as his gaze roved over her. A damn shame. But maybe it would make her less seductive for her male patients.

Turning away, Matt almost groaned aloud at the sudden thought of undressing for a physical examination with Susan Kelly. If she touched him with those long, slender fingers, he'd embarrass himself for sure.

"Just a little overwhelmed," Susan muttered under her breath before smiling at another couple as they stepped forward.

The next person in line brought a smile to Matt's face. "Ah, Jenny, good to see you." Jenny Slater and her husband, Fred, were his neighbors. She, along with Georgy, considered Matt to be her special project. Never having had any children of her own, she kept an eagle eye on Matt, baking him goodies and giving unsolicited advice.

"Where's Fred?" he asked as Susan said goodbye to the other couple. With what he thought was a gasp, Susan seemed to trip and fall against him. He uprighted her, a frown on his face.

"I think maybe we'd better take a break and let you sit down for a while," he said, wondering all the while if this woman was strong enough to be a doctor.

"No, no, I'm fine. I just—just lost my balance." She ignored his look of concern and stuck out her hand to Jenny.

"Hello, I'm Susan Kelly."

"I'm Jenny Slater. So nice to meet you, Doctor. But really, if you're too tired to continue, we'll all understand." Jenny smiled warmly, her motherly instincts coming to the fore.

"No, not at all. I've had to stay on my feet a lot longer when I was an intern. Your husband isn't with you?"

"No, I'm afraid not. One of his prize Guernseys is calving and Fred wouldn't leave her. I hope you won't take offense, but Fred loves his cows."

"Fred and Jenny have the best dairy herd in the state," Matt added. "Fred knows his entire herd by name."

"How can he tell them apart?" Susan asked, a confused look on her face.

Those surrounding her laughed, and Matt watched in admiration as her pale cheeks flushed with color. "City girl," one man muttered and Susan chewed on her bottom lip. He'd noticed she did that when she was stressed.

"Never you mind, dear," Jenny said, patting her arm. "I can't do it, either. Though I do know most of them," she confessed with a sigh. "If I didn't lay down the law, I think Fred would invite them in to eat at the table with us."

"I hope everything goes well for—for the cow this evening, Mrs. Slater," Susan said, smiling at the friendly lady.

"Thank you, dear. And Fred said he'd join us if she delivered right away. But you know how these babies are."

Though Susan smiled at Jenny's last comment, Matt noticed the tension returning to her body. As if Fred joining them meant something to her.

Georgy returned with the glass of water and Susan sipped it gratefully.

"Sure you don't want to take a break?" he whispered, watching her carefully.

"No, let's go ahead and finish. I think I can see the end of the line now." With a stiffening of her shoulders, she determinedly smiled and greeted the next in line.

Even though several of those still waiting to meet the doctor were older men, Matt carefully noted that the tension he'd sensed earlier didn't reoccur. Which meant Fred Slater was the man the doctor was seeking.

Fred Slater.

Matt pictured the older man, his hair gray, his skin leathery. He was a kind man. A lot of men counted Fred Slater their friend. He certainly wasn't a womanizer. But what did he mean to Susan Kelly?

And what would her presence mean to Jenny?

"Mrs. Slater, how long have you lived in Griffin?" Susan asked as she took a bite of potato salad. So much food had been pressed on her when she'd gone through the buffet line, each lady wanting her to try a special recipe. Even if she'd had an appetite, she couldn't have made a dent in the pile on her plate.

And she didn't have an appetite.

Georgy, clearly best friends with Jenny Slater, had invited her to join them for the meal. Susan had expected the mayor to take the opportunity to escape his guardianship of her, but he'd stuck to her side, so the four of them were seated at a small table.

"Oh, all my life," Jenny replied.

"And your husband?"

Though she smiled at Jenny, something in Matt's demeanor drew her attention. He stared at her, menace in his lion eyes, and Susan didn't understand why. Her question had been simple enough.

"Fred was born here, too. He went away to college, but then he came back home."

"How romantic. You waited for him." She knew she shouldn't have made that statement, particularly when she knew that her father hadn't returned at once. But something pushed her to probe for Jenny's response.

"Oh, no," Jenny said with a chuckle. "In fact, Fred was eight years older than me. I hardly knew him. I married John Woody when I graduated. But he was in an accident. We'd only been married two years."

Susan murmured a sympathetic sound, her heart touched by the wistful expression on Jenny's face.

The older woman shrugged off the sympathy. "You never know what turns life will take. I was blessed to find Fred and happiness a second time."

"Fred's devoted to Jenny," Matt added firmly, his eyes still on Susan.

She frowned. What was the matter with him? Did he think she was a temptress, hoping to lure Jenny's husband from her? She almost laughed at the idea.

"Domestic bliss is wonderful," Georgy said, her gaze trained on her nephew. "I've been trying to tell Matt that for several years."

"You forget, Georgy. I tried it. It wasn't so blissful."

Susan looked at him in surprise. "You've been married?"

"Yes. Have you?" he demanded in a counterpunch.

"Yes, briefly." She didn't add anything else. She didn't like to talk about her ill-fated marriage.

"Georgy, you need to work on Dr. Kelly. Not me. She might be more receptive to remarrying." His grim smile wasn't encouraging.

"But, Matt, just the other day, you said it was time you married," Georgy reminded him.

From his expression, Susan thought he not only regretted his aunt's words, he regretted his earlier admission.

"Only if the right woman comes along, Georgy. A woman who wants to work side by side with me on the ranch, who wants a lot of children, who understands country life. Until I find that kind of woman, I'll have to forget marriage."

He shot a look at Susan, as if warning her she didn't qualify. Her chin rose and she smiled coolly at him. "I know what you mean, mayor. Until I find a man who isn't threatened by a wife with a career, who understands that he can't always be first, who is willing to cook his own meals, I won't be remarrying either."

She was disconcerted by the two ladies' response.

"Good for you, Susan," Jenny praised, patting her hand.

"It's about time someone gave as good as they got from my dear nephew," Georgy crowed.

The man glowered at all of them. "Women. You always stick together."

"And men don't?" Susan demanded, determined not to let him have the last word. She wasn't sure why it seemed so important, but it did. Perhaps she was hoping antagonism would lessen the attraction she was trying to fight.

"Only because if we didn't, women would rule the world."

"I think that might be a good thing." Her smile widened at his grimace of frustration.

"And I suppose you became a doctor so you could prove you're just as good as a man?"

His challenge washed over Susan. She'd heard it before in medical school. She'd fought those battles long and hard. But his question reached the core of her, the heart of her determination, and she could only answer honestly.

"No. I became a doctor because I wanted to help people, to relieve the needless suffering if I could, to make life easier for those in pain. That's the only reason I made it through medical school.''

"Commendable," Matt agreed, but before Susan could relax, could feel a dangerous camaraderie with the attractive man opposite her, he asked another question. "And is that the reason you came to Griffin, Dr. Kelly, to help sick people?''

... time to rest. I feel that the body needed a meal to change its chemical value.

Conclusion by ... some agent, which is the same for all of them, could ... in doing this... that all we want... the... therefore had approach... to be of another question... And either the rest you either to... Or... finally to answer... group.

# Chapter Three

Susan wanted to ignore his question.

She couldn't.

Neither could Georgy or Jenny.

"Matt, shame on you!" Georgy said.

"Of course that's why she came," Jenny added, lightly rapping Matt on the arm.

He said nothing, only staring at Susan across the table.

"No," she finally answered. "That's not the reason I came to Griffin." She ignored the way his eyebrows rose above his sunlit eyes, an attitude of having won on his face. "Anywhere I practice medicine, I'll be able to do that." She paused, taking in the worried looks of the two ladies, before adding, "I came to Griffin because I thought I might like it here."

Jenny and Georgy assured her she was right. Still Matt said nothing. Susan stared into his eyes. *He knows. He knows I have another reason for coming here.* But he doesn't know what that reason is, she realized with relief. Her secret was safe. For now.

"How about some dessert, Dr. Kelly?" a lady asked, carrying

a tall, cocoanut cake. "I'm famous for my cakes," she added, beaming at everyone.

"Thank you," Susan replied, relieved at the intrusion that ended their conversation. "But I haven't finished dinner yet. Everything is so delicious." Matt's gaze still rested on her, as if accusing her of lying, even now. She wasn't. The food was delicious, even if it was quite different from that prepared by her grandmother's French chef.

"I'll just cut you a piece and bring it over. Once the others start on my cake, there won't be a crumb left in five minutes flat." She bustled over to the tables and returned only a minute later with a large wedge of cake.

"Thank you. That's—that's quite a large piece."

"Well, I can tell that you're one of us who don't have to worry about our figures." Fortunately, the well-rounded woman didn't wait for an answer as she hurried back to the serving tables.

"She quit worrying a long time ago," Georgy muttered under her breath, and Susan and Jenny exchanged laughing glances.

"Oh, Susan, I do hope you decide to come here. I'm going to enjoy having you around," Jenny said, reaching out again to touch Susan's hand.

Susan was about to agree that she would enjoy Jenny's presence when it suddenly occurred to her that Jenny Slater was her stepmother. She froze.

"Susan? Susan?" Matt called before snapping his fingers in front of her face. "Are you all right?"

"Yes, of course I am." She noted Jenny's withdrawal and hastily added, "Since my mother died, I—I haven't had an older friend, someone I could—I don't mean to imply you're old, Jenny, I mean, Mrs. Slater—" Susan stumbled on, unsure what to say.

"Oh, Susan, I'm flattered, and please, call me Jenny. Everyone does. I was afraid I'd been too forward."

"Jenny adopts all the strays," Georgy said, gently smiling at her friend.

They were interrupted by several members of the City Council, ready to start the little ceremony they'd planned to welcome Susan to Griffin, Texas.

Half an hour later, having received a formal welcome and given a brief speech, Susan said goodnight and left the cafe with Jenny, Georgy and Matt.

"Well, I guess Fred's cow wasn't in a hurry," Georgy said as they stepped into the moonlight.

"They never seem to be," Jenny agreed just as a battered blue pick-up screeched to a halt in front of the cafe. "Oh! There's Fred now."

Jenny left Susan's side to hurry around the front of the truck just as a tall, rangy man got out. She watched him reach out for Jenny, cuddling her against him with a tenderness that wrenched her heart. When she saw Jenny take his hand and tug him in her direction, she stiffened.

She was going to meet her father.

After twenty-four years.

"Susan, I want you to meet my husband, Fred. Honey, this is Dr. Kelly. She's just wonderful." Jenny beamed at everyone, so pleased that her husband had arrived in time to be introduced.

Susan felt as if she'd been turned to stone. In the moonlight, she couldn't see his features clearly. She wanted to reach out to him, to touch him, to seek some forgotten memory. She wanted to claim him as her father. All she could do was stare.

"I'm pleased to meet you, Dr. Kelly. Welcome to Griffin." The man stuck out his hand with no trace of self-consciousness.

Matt's elbow in her side awoke her from her trance and she briefly touched his hand and managed an abrupt nod. She couldn't have spoken if her life had depended on it.

A strong masculine arm came around her shoulders to give support to her wobbly knees. "I'm afraid we about wore her out tonight," Matt assured his old friend. "You know how anxious everyone was to meet her."

"Maybe no one missed me then. Jenny, here, about had a fit when I wouldn't come with her. But Lilah is one of my best heifers and it was her first calf. I couldn't just abandon her."

Susan heard the gentle teasing in his voice, the loving look he cast his wife as he wrapped a long arm around her shoulders, and Susan blinked furiously to hide the moisture filling her eyes. "Of course not." Her low words were stressed, cracking in the middle.

An awkward silence followed before Jenny leaned forward and kissed Susan on her cheek. "We'd better get back. I hope I see you before you leave, dear. Maybe tomorrow."

Her warmth touched Susan and helped her relax just a little. "I'd like that," she whispered in return and then watched as her father and his wife walked to their cars.

Matt's arm fell away as the two vehicles, one driven by Jenny and the other by Fred, pulled away. Susan suddenly felt adrift, missing his strength. The door behind them opened and more of the townspeople exited the cafe, again saying goodbye to Susan. She nodded and smiled, though neither her heart nor her head was in it.

Georgy led the way to Matt's car. Once they were settled inside, Susan again in the front seat beside Matt, Georgy leaned foward and murmured, "You know, Fred wouldn't offend anyone for the world. He and Jenny are fine folk."

"Yes, I'm sure they are. Jenny is—is delightful. I guess I'm just tired. It's been a very long day." She sagged against the comfortable seat, praying Georgy would leave it at that.

With only four blocks to drive, there was no need for conversation. As soon as Matt stopped the car, Susan thanked him for escorting her and introducing her to everyone. She turned to exit the vehicle, but he caught her arm.

"I'm coming in."

His tone left no room for discussion, and the stare he gave her sent shivers up her back. "I—I'm rather tired. Perhaps tomorrow—"

"No. Tonight."

Georgy leaned forward. "Matt, what's the matter with you? There's nothing so pressing that it can't wait until tomorrow."

"Dr. Kelly and I are going to talk tonight, Georgy. We can talk out here, or we can talk in your parlor. We can talk alone, or you can be present, whichever she prefers. But we are going to talk."

Susan held a faint hope that Georgy would order her nephew to leave their guest alone. But even Georgy didn't appear to be proof against the determination in his voice.

"Well, let's get inside, then. If we stay out here, we might melt, all closed up in this car."

Once they were in the cool shadows of the softly lit entry hall, all three came to a halt.

"Well?" Matt asked, staring at her, a question in his eyes.

Susan knew he wanted to know her real reason for coming to Griffin. He'd figured out it had something to do with Fred Slater. His support in her moment of need had told her that. Now he wanted the truth.

She turned to the kind woman beside her. "Georgy, maybe it would be better if I talked to Matt alone. I think I know what's bothering him, and—and it's rather personal."

Georgy's eyebrows soared and her gaze darted between the two of them. Too late, Susan realized the older woman might have a different interpretation than the truth.

With a wide grin, Georgy gave her a brief hug, warned her nephew not to keep Susan up too late, and scurried up the stairs before Susan could think of anything to say to correct her false impression.

Matt's grim look confirmed her mistake, but he just gestured to the parlor and stood back for her to precede him.

One lamp glowed, casting shadows about the large room. Perhaps it was best that Matt not be able to see her too clearly, she thought, as she moved as far away from him as the room allowed.

Matt had other ideas, however. When she turned around, he was beside her, his broad frame only scant inches away.

"Not even for the sake of having a doctor in Griffin will I allow you to hurt Jenny Slater."

"I don't want to hurt Jenny," Susan protested, her eyes widening as she looked up at him.

Even in the dim light, those blue eyes, filled with some unexplained emotion, spoke to Matt, promising more than any woman could possibly deliver.

"You've got some connection to Fred Slater that Jenny doesn't know about." He wasn't going to be taken in by her innocent pose.

"Why do you say that?"

"Don't play games with me. I think I deserve the truth. After all, you're here at our expense to interview. Not to look up old friends . . . or enemies." He spun around and paced across the room. If he stayed that close to her for much longer, he might accept any excuse she gave him.

"I am interviewing. That's what the reception was about this evening. Didn't I perform to your expectations?"

Her chin lifted in challenge and his fingers itched to caress the expanse of white throat it revealed. Almost groaning aloud, he cleared his throat. He had to get hold of himself. He wasn't some kid just out of high school turned on by every skirt he saw. "You know everyone was pleased. Hell, you could've spit in their faces and they would offer you the job."

"Then I don't think you have anything to complain about. I certainly didn't spit in anyone's face."

She was stonewalling him, but he was sure he was right. She was here because of Fred Slater. "I realized you were overqualified for what we were offering. But I don't think it's fair to raise everyone's hopes when you have no intention of accepting the job."

"I never said I had no intention of accepting the job. That's your imagination working overtime."

"So you're considering it? Seriously?" He stared at her, trying to keep his glare in place.

She couldn't return his look. As her gaze shifted away from him, he was filled with disgust. As beautiful as she was, like Lindsay, she was rotten inside. She'd pulled a dirty trick on a town which had worked too hard to be treated this way. He turned to stalk from the room.

"Matt, he's my father." Her whispered words stopped him as nothing else could.

Spinning around, he stared at her. "What did you say?"

"Fred Slater is my father." Her words were softer now, as if she were tasting them for the first time.

"Kelly's your married name? Why didn't you say something?" He'd known Fred Slater all his life. He knew there'd been an early marriage, before he married Jenny, but he'd never heard there was a child.

"It's a long story. And tonight wasn't the right time to tell him who I am."

She stood there, fragile and trembling, her eyes wide with fatigue and a hint of fear. All he could think of was his desire to pick her up and cuddle her, comfort her, until she, too, acknowledged the desire that filled him every minute he was near her, in spite of what he thought about her behavior.

To hide that need, he snapped at her. "Sit down and tell me. I've got all night."

She obeyed but remained silent. He joined her on the sofa, but he kept some distance between them, hoping his rioting hormones would calm down. A thick curtain of dark hair hid her face from him as she leaned forward.

"Are you saying Fred doesn't know he has a daughter?"

She shook her head no. "He knows. He left when I was three."

"Fred Slater just walked away from his own child? I don't believe that, Dr. Kelly. You saw him tonight, worried over a cow. You saw him with Jenny. You think I'll believe he'd walked away from his own flesh and blood?"

Her back stiffened and she threw her head up. "Yes. I'll admit there were difficult circumstances. But he did leave."

He stared at her fragile features, surprised to discover a slight resemblance to Fred. A little calmer, he asked, "What circumstances?"

"I don't think you have a right to know that. It's between my father and myself." She turned away, her voice dying to a whisper, as if just calling the man her father was overwhelming.

"Jenny doesn't know?" he asked, wondering what the information would do to Fred's wife.

"I—I don't really know. Was his earlier marriage a secret?"

"No. I vaguely remember mention of it. But it's not talked about. Everyone loves Jenny. They wouldn't do or say anything that would make her uncomfortable."

"She's a lovely person."

There was an awkward silence before he returned to the aspect of their conversation that was truly his province. "So you really had no intention of becoming our doctor?"

"No! No. I—I didn't know. I thought I could see him, talk to him, and then decide. I *might* want to stay here, near him."

He heard the doubt in her words as clearly as if she'd told him she was returning to Dallas.

"It was unfair to accept our offer and have no intention of agreeing to it." He got up from the sofa to pace across the room.

"It's an interview, not a promise," she insisted, her voice growing stronger. "And I *am* considering it. I'm just—just confused right now."

The quiet of a country night settled over the room as Matt stared out the parlor window at the empty streets of Griffin. Any indignation he was feeling about her behavior was laced with large dollops of desire. And that irritated him. She wasn't what he needed.

"What are you going to do?" he demanded, his back still to her.

"I don't know."

"I mean about Fred."

When she said nothing, he turned around and advanced toward her, wanting to be close enough to see her face in the dim light.

"I'm going to talk to him." Her words were whispered and her face was again shielded by a curtain of long hair.

"When?"

"I don't know. I don't have a car."

"How about in the morning? I'll drive you out to his place."

Her head snapped up and he read a sudden fear in her eyes that had him sucking in his breath, fighting the need to comfort her. "I—I don't want to put you to any more trouble.

"I represent the town. You came here, at our expense, to consider accepting our offer. Until you talk to Fred, that won't happen."

She rose from the sofa, drifting across the room in a distracted fashion, her arms clasped about her. He fought the longing to reach for her, pull her against him.

*Damn it, man, think with your head, not your body!*

"Very well. I'll go talk to him in the morning. If you're sure you don't mind driving me. I could rent a car—"

"We don't have a car rental agency in Griffin," he said. This woman had no idea what living in a small town was like. There was no way she'd ever work out here.

Maybe it was for the best. She wasn't what he needed, he reminded himself again. But he wasn't sure he could convince his hormones of that. "I'll pick you up at nine in the morning."

"All right," she agreed in a soft voice, turning her back to him again.

"You never did explain why you waited until now to contact your father." He watched her carefully.

Susan sighed and rubbed her hands over her arms, as if she were cold. "Mother died six months ago. I—I found letters from my father that I'd never received. I thought he'd just gone away and never cared what happened to me."

He circled her, anxious to see her face. Her eyes were shadowed, but a single tear escaped one and wended its way down her soft cheek.

"I'll get Georgy to invite Jenny over for coffee in the morning, and I'll take you to see Fred. Maybe, that way, we can spare Jenny the shock your revelation might be."

Her teeth chewed on her bottom lip, but she said nothing, only nodding.

He stiffened his resolve and walked away without touching her. There was nothing left to say. She'd see her father and then she'd leave. They'd have to find another doctor, but it might be best for everyone concerned.

# Chapter Four

Matt rubbed his eyes wearily after he'd slid behind the wheel of his jeep. He'd been up at sunrise, following his usual schedule, but he'd tossed and turned most of the night thinking about his talk with Susan Kelly. He was worried about Fred and Jenny. What would the revelation of Susan's identity do to them?

Even when he was able to put aside those questions and concerns, he was left with the attraction he felt toward the doctor. She'd knocked him for a loop from the very beginning. He'd seen beautiful women before. Hell, he'd been married to one. But none of them drew him like Susan.

This morning, he assured himself, he was back to reality. Susan Kelly was nothing to him and must remain nothing to him. She was a career woman. He needed a woman who would make him her career.

He'd turned thirty-four his last birthday. That was when he'd made the decision to remarry. And he had several candidates in mind, strong, healthy women who would produce strong sons. Women who understood country life, who wouldn't leave when things got difficult. Women whose faces he couldn't call to mind as long as he was near Susan Kelly.

With a sigh, he started the engine and headed for town and his aunt's house, only five minutes away.

"Why, good morning, Matt. I didn't know you were coming to call this morning," Georgy said, a big smile on her face, as she answered the door herself. " 'Course, maybe I should've guessed since you and Susan spent some time alone last night."

Matt ignored the speculative grin on her face. "I need you to do me a favor, Georgy."

"You want me to tell Susan how great you are? No problem. I've already been—"

"Georgy, this is important." His grim expression must have pierced her exhuberant imagination, because she sobered and frowned at him.

"I want you to call Jenny and ask her to come have a cup of coffee with you and Susan." Though she looked surprised at his request, she nodded in agreement. "Then, when Jenny arrives, tell her Susan was called away."

"What? Why would I do that?"

"I need to take Susan to—to a meeting."

"Then why call Jenny in the first place?"

Susan appeared in the doorway leading to the dining room. "Because I need to talk to Fred Slater privately, Georgy," she said. Georgy spun around to stare at her. "I'm afraid I haven't been quite honest with you. I knew Fred in Dallas a—a long time ago, and I have a message for him that might upset Jenny."

"I don't want Jenny hurt," Georgy protested, looking first at Susan and then her nephew.

Before Matt could say anything, Susan stepped over and took Georgy's hand. "I don't want Jenny hurt either. That's why it will be better if she's not there. Then it will be up to Fred to tell her what he thinks is best."

Georgy studied Susan's face for several minutes and Matt held his breath. No one fooled his aunt easily. Did she believe

Susan? He didn't see how anyone could resist Susan's bright blue gaze, but then, his aunt wasn't a man.

"Okay. I'll go call her. Do I have to tell her you'll be here?"

"Not if you think she'll come just for a chat."

Georgy paused to think, then shook her head. "Probably not. She said yesterday she's behind on a lot of things right now." Georgy headed for the kitchen, leaving Susan and Matt alone in the entry hall.

"You handled that well," he murmured, his gaze roving over her, touching her as he wished he could. She was dressed in tan slacks tailored to her trim figure and a white knit top, its short sleeves and shoulders crocheted to give enticing glimpses of her soft skin.

"I had a lot of time last night to think since I wasn't able to sleep."

Now that she'd mentioned it, he noted the faint circles under her eyes. At least he wasn't the only one to suffer. He couldn't help wondering if he'd played a role in her sleeplessness, or if she'd only been concerned with facing her father.

"You braided your hair again," he muttered before he could stop himself.

"It's cooler this way."

Before he could make any more inane statements that might reveal how easily she confused him, Georgy returned. "She was real pleased with the invitation," she said, obviously unhappy with the lies she'd just told. "She'll be here in about fifteen minutes."

Again Susan reached out for Georgy's hand. "I really appreciate it, Georgy. I wouldn't ask you to do this if it wasn't important."

The older woman nodded but continued to frown.

"When I can, I'll explain everything," Susan added, "but I don't know when that will be. It's up to Fred Slater as to whether anyone else is told."

"I understand," Georgy said, squeezing her hand. "Are

you all right? I thought you were acting a little uptight this morning.''

Matt watched in bemusement as Susan's eyes filled with unshed tears and Georgy reached out to embrace her.

"Thank you for—for caring, Georgy. I'll be fine,'' Susan assured her, pulling back from the embrace.

Briskly, to hide her emotions, Georgy said, "Then you two had better skedaddle or Jenny will get here before you can get away.''

Matt led Susan out the door with only a thank you to his aunt. He was surprised at how quickly Georgy had accepted Susan. Normally his aunt was slow to let anyone get close to her.

"You and Georgy seem to be getting along well,'' he commented as he turned down a side street and parked.

Susan looked at him, confused. "Why are we stopping?''

"We have to let Jenny drive past. If she sees you with me, she'll suspect Georgy lied to her. Georgy would be upset about that. She prides herself on her honesty.''

Susan nodded her understanding but said nothing else.

"You didn't answer my question.''

"What question?''

He raised his eyebrows at her stubbornness. "I commented on how well you and Georgy are getting along.''

"That wasn't a question, but, yes, we are enjoying each other.'' She didn't look at him.

"I guess you're finding all the Griffins easy to charm,'' he said, irritated that she was trying to brush off his attempts at conversation.

"Somehow I don't think I'd describe your reaction last night as charmed.'' There was an edge to her words and she flashed him a glare before looking away again.

At least she didn't seem to realize just how much she had affected him. He'd rather not advertise the attraction he was determined to get over.

In his rearview mirror, he saw Jenny's car go by. "There's Jenny. We can go now."

"Are—are the Slaters well off?"

He frowned and stopped the jeep, looking at her. "Why?"

"I just wondered."

"If you think you're going to hit Fred up to pay your school loans or something, you can—"

"No! Forget it. Just—just take me to see him."

He did as she asked, since he couldn't think of anything else to do. He hadn't answered her question, but Fred could afford to do what he wanted. His land was paid for and he and Jenny made a nice income.

If Susan Kelly tried to get money out of Fred, he'd help him fight her. Griffin didn't need a golddigger as their doctor. And he didn't need anymore of a headache than he already had.


Susan remained silent the rest of the ride. She'd already messed up. Her one attempt to get information about her father had convinced the man next to her that she was after Fred Slater's money. It was ironic that she would be accused of the very thing her grandmother had accused her father.

She supposed she could convince Matt Griffin of her innocence by telling him of her inheritance, but she refused to do so. She'd been married once for her family's money, and she didn't need to make herself any more vulnerable to the sexy man beside her.

Her grandmother and mother's estates ensured that she'd never have to work a day in her life. In fact, she was sure she couldn't live long enough to spend all her inheritance, even if she tried.

Until her mother's death, she hadn't realized just how much money there was. They'd always lived extremely well, but her grandmother had kept her finances private. After her grandmother's death, her mother had left everything up to the lawyers.

Susan hadn't understood some of her husband's remarks or

his attempt to forestall the divorce, until her mother's death. He had hoped to have part of her inheritance. But the divorce had been final almost two years ago. Now, Susan was still trying to understand the enormity of her inheritance, as well as to make important decisions about her future.

Matt turned off the paved road onto a gravel drive that led to a neat, well-tended frame house. Surrounded by trees, unusual in west Texas, the place looked cool and inviting. Several sheds and small buildings were behind the house, and two large barns were just within the fenced pasture.

As he stopped the jeep, Matt pressed down on the horn.

"Why did you do that?"

"Because Fred isn't going to be sitting in the living room waiting for a guest. He's out working. That's to let him know he's got company."

Even as he finished speaking, Susan saw a tall form step out of the first barn. Matt got out and waved and Fred Slater started toward them.

Susan couldn't move. The moment of truth had arrived. What was she going to say? She'd spent half the night trying to prepare, but all she'd done was go in circles. Perhaps she should've left well enough alone and stayed in Dallas. But it was too late to have such thoughts now.

"Hi, Matt. Didn't expect to see you today," Fred Slater said, extending his hand.

"I've brought the doctor out for a visit." Matt's voice was stiff. He was uncomfortable with the role he was playing, but Susan reminded herself it was by his choice.

"Oh? I thought Jenny was gonna go have coffee at Georgy's with the doc. I must've gotten confused." Her father's weathered face wore a warm smile, and Susan craved that smile for herself. But she didn't think he'd be quite so congenial when he knew why she was there.

Matt turned to look at her. Susan opened the car door and got out. Drawing a deep breath, she raised her eyes to her father's and said, "I wanted to talk to you without Jenny present. Could—could we go inside?"

Fred frowned, his gaze darting from Susan to Matt and back again as he hesitantly agreed to her suggestion. He led the way into the house and gestured for Susan and Matt to sit down.

As nervous as she was, Susan still recognized Jenny's personality in the practical yet welcoming furnishings. Two comfortable sofas in a jade green print with touches of pink and a darker green were enhanced by soft pink drapes. There was an aura of warmth and happiness that reminded her of Jenny's smile.

"There's nothing wrong with Jenny, is there? I mean, she's not sick. She seemed just fine this morning, 'cept for being a little tired, but it's been awfully hot lately and—"

"Mr. Slater, I'm not here about Jenny. I—I have something to tell you. I'm afraid it will be a shock to you. If you'll sit down—"

He did so and gestured for her to continue.

There was no easy way to confront this man with his past. Susan's gaze remained fixed on him, hungering for some memory, some response that would give her a clue to his feelings.

"My mother—my mother was Elizabeth Manton."

Her words hung in the air as Fred stared at her, his skin paling. When Susan saw recognition and an incredible joy in his eyes, she couldn't breathe. All her hopes would be realized if this man could accept her as his daughter.

"Susan? You're my Susan?"

Before she could even acknowledge his incredulous question, he'd leaped from his chair and pulled her into his arms. Tears filled Susan's eyes as she wrapped her arms around him, and some distant memory told her she'd done so before.

Unfortunately, she recognized almost to the second when the shock wore off and Fred Slater returned to reality. His arms slackened around her and he took a step back. She raised her tear-streaked face, fearing what she'd see in his.

"You really are Susan."

"Yes," she whispered, her heart pleading with him to not retreat from the warmth of their embrace.

"Why are you here?"

The tightness of his words, his shuttered gaze, told her he was withdrawing from her. She swiped away the tears with the back of her hand and sank her teeth into her bottom lip. When she had herself under control, she said quietly, "I—I wanted to see you. And interview for the position, also," she hurriedly added, remembering Matt's presence.

"You really are a doctor?"

"Yes."

"Your grandmother must've hated that." There was a bitterness in his voice that stabbed her.

"Yes, she did."

"Your mother?"

"She died just after Christmas."

He turned away from her and crossed the room to stare out the window. "I'm sorry." He said nothing else until Susan cleared her throat. Then he turned to look at her. "And now that you're out of family, assuming your grandmother is dead, you thought you'd look me up?"

There was no welcome in his voice, none of the joy she'd momentarily seen in his eyes. He was angry.

She couldn't blame him for his anger nor deny his words. But there was more to the story. Unconsciously, she stiffened, wiping all emotion from her voice as she answered his question. "Not exactly."

He practically leaped across the room. Before Susan could move, Matt was beside her, a hand against Fred Slater's chest.

"Take it easy, man. Give her a chance to explain."

She was surprised by his support. It provided the only warmth in the room.

"You don't understand," Fred raged. "She sounded just like her damned grandmother, cold, calculating. The woman ruined my life! She drove me from my wife and child. She made me feel like a failure! I couldn't—'' He sobbed and turned his back on the other two.

Susan's tears overflowed down her cheeks again. She hadn't wanted to hurt this man, her father. His letters, the ones she'd found and read, had been filled with love. But they'd also shown shame and anger, though those emotions were carefully concealed.

Matt had left her side to comfort his friend. She stared at the backs of the two men. Finally, she whispered, ''If I could just explain—''

Fred released a deep shudder before turning to her. ''My apologies . . . Susan. There's no need to explain. You were only three when I left. None of it was your fault.'' His face was closed, trying to hide his embarrassment at his breakdown behind chiseled features.

''I—I never received your letters,'' she hurriedly said, fearing he would ask her to leave if she didn't speak quickly. ''I only found them after Mother's death.''

There was a flare of something in his eyes, blue like her own, but she feared it was anger again. She rushed on. ''I wanted you to know that I would have written to you, visited you, if I'd known.''

''I see.''

His minimal response did nothing to encourage Susan. He was shutting her out, treating her with the politeness of a stranger. She almost preferred his anger.

''It was kind of you to come explain to me. I'll admit I was hurt by your lack of response. It never occurred to me that your mother would do such a thing.'' He had himself well in hand now. Susan recognized the stubbornness that settled over his features. Her grandmother had accused her of the same thing often enough.

''Mother was always controlled by Grandmother.''

He only nodded, leaving an awkward silence.

Matt shifted his feet. ''I'm sure you two have a lot to discuss. Would you like me to wait outside?''

"No!" Both responded, then looked away from each other.

"You knew about this?" Fred's words were razor sharp.

"Not until last night," Matt hastily assured him.

Susan sank down on the sofa, relieved that her wobbly knees didn't have to continue to hold her up. What should she say now?

Before she could speak, Fred also sat down and said, "I'm pleased you're doing so well."

Another polite remark, easily made to a stranger. Though she kept her face passive, her heart shed tears. "Yes, I'm doing well. I finished my internship a month ago."

"Of course. That's why you're here, to interview—wait a minute. They said you were Dr. Kelly. Where did you get that name?"

"I'm divorced."

He turned away from her, making it impossible to read his thoughts. She waited for him to speak.

"And you're considering practicing medicine here in Griffin?" There was an incredulity in his voice that didn't please her.

"Yes."

"Why? I'd bet you've never lived anywhere but Dallas. You're not used to a small town. It would never work."

Matt heaved a sigh. "I'm afraid you're right. It's unfortunate. We've gone to an awful lot of trouble to get us a doctor."

"But there must be other doctors—" Fred insisted.

"Would it be so terrible for me to move here?" Susan whispered, getting to the heart of her father's argument.

He only glanced at her before turning away. "For what purpose? Our time has passed, Susan. You're an adult. I'm sorry for the past, but I can't change it."

She bowed her head, hoping to hide the tears.

"And I damned well won't let that woman ruin my life a second time."

"I don't want to ruin your life," Susan cried, wounded that he would think such a thing.

"Not you, child, your grandmother. Why did you make sure Jenny wasn't here?" Before she could pull herself together, he answered his own question. "Because she might be hurt by what you came to tell me. Jenny is—is the best thing that ever happened to me. The only thing that saddens her is the fact that she's never been able to give me children."

He stood again and paced the floor. "She's never understood that she's more than enough to fill my life with joy. She knows I have a daughter, but you're not part of my life. If you move here, as my daughter, it would be a constant reminder of what she considers her failure." He swung around to face Susan. "I know *I* failed you. I live with that failure every day. But my loyalty, my love, my life, is for Jenny now. I can't acknowledge you as my child without hurting her."

Susan stood, her heart breaking, and tried to memorize her father's face through her tears. "I understand. Jenny is special. I'm grateful you let me explain and I—I hope you and Jenny will be very happy."

"If you need anything, or if I can help you—" Fred offered, an awkwardness in his voice.

"No," Susan managed but could say no more.

As she turned to walk out of his life as abruptly as she'd entered it, a warm voice rang through the house.

"Fred? Are you in here? I'm home."

# Chapter Five

Matt wasn't sure who gasped, but all three of them stared at each other in consternation.

Jenny's voice continued as she came through the house. "Is that Matt's truck out front? Fred?"

She stepped into the living room before anyone found a voice to answer her. "Why, Susan! What are you—" Jenny's breathless words faded as her eyes rolled back in her head and she fainted dead away.

Fred reached Jenny first, before she could hit the floor, folding her against his chest. "Jenny? Jenny? What's wrong, honey?"

"Put her on the sofa," a crisp voice ordered, and Matt had to turn around to believe that it was Susan who had spoken. The emotionally distraught young woman he'd watched with a heavy heart the past few minutes was gone, replaced by a doctor.

Fred instinctively obeyed the authority in her voice and stepped back as Susan felt for Jenny's pulse. The two men stood silently while she checked Jenny out. Before she told them anything, Jenny stirred.

"Wh-what happened?" she asked weakly.

"You fainted," Susan said gently. She turned to her father. "We need to take Jenny to the clinic so I can do a thorough examination. Matt, would you call one of the nurses available and ask her to meet us there?"

"Hurry," Fred urged, fear that something might be wrong with his wife written on his face.

"Right," Matt agreed, slipping from the room. When he returned, Jenny was arguing about the need to go to town.

"Sweetheart, we need to do what the doctor says," Fred insisted.

"Nonsense," Jenny protested, sitting up too quickly. She fell back against the cushions, a startled expression on her face. "I—I don't feel too good."

"Just take it easy, Jenny. I'm sure it's nothing serious, but we'd rather be safe than sorry," Susan said with a warm, reassuring smile.

Matt decided Susan earned an "A" in bedside manner. Both Jenny and Fred were reassured, but Susan was getting her way. Fred scooped Jenny up to carry her out to Matt's vehicle, and he and Susan followed.

"Maybe we should go in our car, so we'll have a way back," Fred suggested in a distracted manner.

"Don't worry about it, Fred. I'll bring you both back later," Matt assured them. He took Jenny from Fred so he could climb into the back seat. Then he handed the petite Jenny in to her husband.

"This is silly. I can at least sit up," Jenny protested weakly.

"Humor us, Jenny," Susan suggested, a teasing note in her voice, though Matt thought she looked serious. "It makes the guys feel better to think they're helping by hauling you around."

During the ten minute ride into town, Matt expected everyone to remain silent, tense, but Susan initiated a rambling conversation into which she inserted several casual questions about Jenny's health.

"It really is hot out here, isn't it? I guess because there are so few trees, it seems hotter. Does the heat bother you, Jenny?"

"No more than anyone else," Jenny said with a weak smile.

"It exhausts me. I guess I'll get used to it. Fred said you've been tired lately," Susan commented, "but then I imagine you work hard every day. Life on a farm isn't easy."

"No," Jenny said slowly. "But I have been a little more tired than usual. Do you think it's my heart, Susan? Do you think I'm really sick? I don't want to be a burden to Fred!" The rising anxiety in her voice caught everyone's attention.

"Don't be silly, Jenny," Susan chided in just the right tones to soothe her. "I'd be yelling at Matt to drive faster if anything was really wrong. Instead, I'm tempted to ask him to slow down. I think he has fantasies about being a race car driver."

Jenny gave a half laugh, half sob. "I've warned him about driving too fast. He's much better now than when he was a teenager."

"I'm glad I didn't know him then," Susan said with a mock shudder.

Jenny's soft chuckle was her reward. "He was a handful, but he's only gotten better, so you didn't miss too much."

Matt turned into a parking space in front of the clinic. "You two can stop examining my past life, if you don't mind. We're here now."

The nurse Matt had called, Kay, was waiting at the door and led the way into an examining room. Fred lay Jenny down on the examining table.

"If you two gentlemen will step into the waiting area, we'll get started," Susan suggested, a calm smile on her face.

"I want to stay with Jenny," Fred protested, holding on to his wife's hand.

"I appreciate your concern, but it will go more quickly if you wait outside. I promise she's in no danger." Susan's words were firm but friendly.

Matt met her gaze and obeyed her silent command. "Come on, Fred, let's let them do their jobs. I'm sure we put some new magazines in that waiting room.'' He led his friend away from his wife.

Georgy had done a nice job of the decor of the waiting room. Soothing blues dominated, though the color didn't seem to be working on Fred as he paced back and forth.

''Do you think she knows what she's doing?'' he asked once as he passed by Matt, sitting on one of the sofas.

''Yeah. Her record's impressive. Besides, you heard her say she doesn't think anything's seriously wrong. But if you're not happy with her diagnosis, you can take Jenny to San Angelo this afternoon.''

Fred paced for a few more minutes. Then he sat down beside Matt. ''I think I was kind of hard on her.''

''Jenny?''

''No. Susan.''

Matt said nothing.

''She surprised me. No, shocked me. She shocked me. I— I'd never expected to hear from her again.'' He rubbed his face. ''She's—she's beautiful, isn't she?''

''No doubt about it. Must not look much like her old man,'' Matt teased.

''Her mother was a beauty. But weak. Nothing like Jenny.'' He jerked up from the sofa. ''She's got to be all right. I can't live without her.''

The anguish in Fred's voice disturbed Matt. He didn't know what to do to help him. But he had to try. ''Susan said it wasn't serious, Fred.''

''I know. I hope she meant what she said.'' Fred paced back across the room, then sat beside Matt again. ''Jenny means everything to me. She's more than beautiful. She's—she's perfect!''

Matt patted Fred on the shoulder as he leaned forward to bury his face in his hands. ''Susan's a good doctor, Fred. She'll fix Jenny up.''

"She's not going to stay, is she?" Fred suddenly asked.

Matt didn't have to ask who he was talking about now. He shrugged his shoulders. "I kind of doubt it."

"I didn't mean to mess things up for the town, Matt. You know I didn't. But I couldn't hurt Jenny!"

"It's all right, Fred. I understand." And he did. But the entire town was going to be devastated at their failure to convince Susan to stay. And they'd have to start their search all over again.

He'd expected this outcome last night, even welcomed it, because of the strong attraction he felt for her. Now Matt knew he was wrong. Susan was a good doctor. He was convinced of that. But even more, she'd shown courage today and a quiet dignity that had impressed him. Even if she wasn't what he was looking for in a wife, he admired Dr. Susan Kelly, and her departure would be the town's loss.


"Kay, would you help Jenny dress now?" Susan asked pleasantly. Her incredulous suspicions had been confirmed, and she tried to contain her excitement until Jenny was ready to talk to her.

She sat on the stool provided for the doctor and made several notations on the empty chart Kay had handed her. The town had done a wonderful job of equipping the clinic. All it needed was someone to operate it.

What she had to tell Jenny made it even more important that they have a doctor. But she wasn't going to be that person. After her talk with her father, staying here was impossible.

"I'm dressed, Susan," Jenny said softly, worry lining her forehead.

Susan spun around, her own concerns put away for another time. "Don't look so worried, Jenny."

"But what's wrong? Why did I faint? I've never done that before."

"But then, you've never had this condition before. Do you know what's wrong with you, Jenny?" Susan asked, unable to resist the question.

"Am I anemic? I always eat right, Susan, and I take vitamin pills with iron."

"No, Jenny, you're not anemic, though I will be giving you some more vitamins to take. Jenny," Susan drew a deep breath, "I think this will be happy news. You're pregnant."

Fortunately, Jenny was sitting down, because she fainted again. Susan and Kay caught her before she fell out of the chair.

"Oh, dear," Kay muttered and broke open a capsule of smelling salts handily stored on the nearby cabinet. She waved it beneath Jenny's nose and brought her to at once.

"Jenny, you've got to stop doing that," Susan teased. "I hesitate to ask, but do you remember my diagnosis?" She kept a firm grip on Jenny's arms in case she passed out again.

"You can't be serious," Jenny said, breathing shallowly. "That's impossible."

"Why is it impossible?"

Her cheeks flushing bright red, Jenny said, "Well, I mean, it's possible, of course. I mean, Fred and I—well, we've been married almost twenty years. I thought I couldn't—how could it happen?"

"Have you used contraceptives?"

"No. We *wanted* children. Desperately. There was no reason to use them."

"Did you ever have an examination to see if there was a problem?" Susan asked curiously.

Jenny looked away. "No. You see, Fred has a daughter from his first marriage, so we knew he could—could father a child. I figured it was me. I—I didn't want anyone to tell me I couldn't hope."

Susan avoided her gaze. "Well, your hoping has paid off. In about six and a half months, you and Fred will have your first child." And she would have a brother or sister, Susan suddenly realized. All during childhood, she'd wished for a sibling, someone to talk to, to play with, even to fight with, like most of her friends had. Like Jenny, she shouldn't have given up hope.

"Susan," Jenny suddenly asked, reaching out to grip Susan's arm, "Is everything all right? I'm forty-two years old."

"I know, but you're in very good health, Jenny. At forty-two, you fall into what is called a high-risk pregnancy, but as far as I can tell, you're fine. In a couple of weeks, you can schedule an amniocentesis test in San Angelo. You'll know more when you get the results from that."

Reassured, Jenny stared into to space, cradling her stomach with her hands. "A baby." As if Susan had snapped her fingers, Jenny awakened from her trance. "Fred! I've got to tell Fred!"

"Easy does it, Jenny. You've got to stop rushing around, or I'll be picking you up off the floor again."

"But can I go tell Fred?"

"Of course. I'll go with you. I'm sure he's going to have some questions, too." She nodded to Kay, who was tidying up the room. "I'll be back in a minute."

When the two of them entered the waiting room, arm in arm, the men leaped from the sofa and raced across the room to greet them.

"Sweetheart? Are you all right? Doctor, what's wrong with her?" Fred demanded of both of them.

Susan refused to let her own feelings ruin the moment. It didn't matter that her father was treating her as a stranger. At least not much. His wife was about to make him very happy.

"Fred, you won't believe it! It's—it's a miracle. We're going to have a baby!" Jenny informed him, her face glowing with excitement.

The four of them stood frozen in time, waiting for Jenny's words to sink into Fred. When they did, he erupted with a joy that matched his wife's. Swinging her into his arms, he spun about the room, shouting, "A baby! We're going to have a baby."

"I don't recommend that kind of treatment for pregnant ladies," Susan advised. "You'll be lucky if she doesn't throw up her breakfast."

Fred immediately halted his celebration and allowed his wife's feet to touch the floor again, though he kept her in his arms. "I didn't hurt you, Jenny? You're all right?"

"I'm fine, Fred. I'm incredibly fine," she assured him before she burst into tears.

Both Matt and Fred turned to stare at Susan, as if she'd tricked them. She moved forward. "Jenny's emotions are a little unpredictable right now. It's all due to the hormonal changes she's going through. Don't be alarmed."

"Is that why she's been crying more lately?" Fred asked, wonder reappearing in his eyes.

After seeing the pain her father had suffered from the birth of his first child, her, Susan was happy that he could enjoy this moment to the fullest. She wanted her father, Jenny and the precious child she was carrying to be able to celebrate their happiness together.

"Yes, that's why."

"Everything's all right?" Matt asked in a low voice as Fred turned back to mopping up Jenny's tears. But he heard Matt's question and looked at Susan sharply.

"She's fine. It's a high-risk pregnancy at her age, but I think everything will be okay."

"You mean that?" Fred demanded.

"I mean that," she assured him.

"Isn't it wonderful?" Jenny asked, sunshine peaking through her tears as she smiled. "Susan came here just in time. She'll help me get through this."

Susan said nothing. As much as she wanted to have a role in this new baby's life, she knew she couldn't. Her heart ached with a longing she had to withstand. There was no place for her in her father's life or in Griffin, Texas.

"Sweetheart, I don't think—we can't expect Dr. Kelly to move here just for us. I'm sure she has many offers."

"But—" Jenny began, agitation clear on her face.

"Jenny, the important thing is your baby, and you need to stay calm. Even if I'm not your regular doctor, I want the best for both of you. And I recommend a two hour rest every afternoon with your feet up." She smiled at Jenny but couldn't look at her father.

"Yes," Jenny agreed with a deep sigh. "It would just be so nice if you—"

Susan broke away from Jenny's beseeching gaze, looking at Matt for assistance. She couldn't continue to say no when her heart wanted to accept. Here was the family she'd always wanted, filled with warmth and love. At least the baby would have that caring. Maybe her father would even permit her to visit, once the child was here, to play a remote role in their lives.

"Susan's right, Jenny," Matt agreed. "You've got to think about your baby. I'll worry about finding a doctor for you." He gave Fred, still holding Jenny, a slap on the back. "Are you two ready to head for home?"

"Yeah. Is there anything else we should do, Doctor? Besides the nap, I mean," Fred asked.

Susan tried to conceal how much her father's formality hurt. He acted as if their earlier talk hadn't happened. Drawing a deep breath, she decided he was right. Pretending they weren't related was probably the best thing to do. "I could give you a prescription for vitamins. Other than that, you'd best wait until Jenny chooses her doctor."

She turned to go back to the examining room where Kay would have the proper forms. "I'll be right back with the prescription."

And hopefully more composure, she thought. The tears that formed in her eyes couldn't be blamed on hormonal changes as Jenny's could. They were caused by an aching heart.

The nurse had the examining room spotless again.

"You've done a nice job, Kay. Thank you for coming on such short notice. Do we have any prescription forms?"

"Yes, Doctor. And I enjoyed working with you. I hope you decide to come here. The town is anxious to have you, and Mrs. Slater is going to need a doctor nearby."

Susan only smiled at the nurse. There was nothing she could say. Or do. Nothing at all.

"Have you made up your mind yet?" Kay pressed.

Unable to avoid a direct answer, Susan said aloud what she already knew. "I don't think I'm going to be able to accept the town's offer, Kay. I'd like to, but—there are reasons why I can't."

The nurse's hopeful expression disappeared, replaced by sadness. "I'm sorry. I thought you fit in so well."

"I'm sorry, too."

"Maybe you could stay for a little while. You know, try us out on a temporary basis, and see if those reasons disappear."

Susan stared at the nurse, struck by what she'd said. Could she? Could she stay for, say, six months, maybe seven, just until Jenny's baby is born? Would her father allow her to do that, as long as she didn't reveal her identity?

No one was waiting for her in Dallas, or anywhere else for that matter. If she didn't set up a practice at once, it wouldn't affect her financially. She could stay until they found a doctor they were happy with.

If her father . . . and Matt . . . would agree.

She wrote out the prescription, told Kay goodbye, and returned to the waiting room.

Fred promised to hurry to the drug store and have the vitamins filled at once. Matt offered to escort Jenny to his jeep for the ride home. Before they could leave, however, Susan leaned over to whisper in his ear.

"I need to talk to you."

"About what?" he questioned, a frown on his brow.

"Could you come to Georgy's after you take them home?"

His golden-eyed gaze tried to see inside her and Susan wondered if he could. There was a rising excitement in her as she thought about staying, even for a limited time, using her medical skills to care for her own sibling. And other reasons. She ducked her head away from his penetrating gaze.

"Give me half an hour," he muttered and escorted Jenny out the door.

# Chapter Six

Since Georgy's was only a couple of blocks from the clinic, Susan walked back, her thoughts on the idea of staying in Griffin temporarily until they found a doctor.

The only difficulty would be her father. Susan slowed her pace as she forced herself to be honest. Matt Griffin was also a problem. She found herself attracted to the man. So much so that she was always aware of him. It irritated her. But she could overcome distractions. She'd done it before.

Georgy stepped out of the parlor as Susan entered.

"Well, did you talk to Fred?"

It was almost noon, three hours since Susan had left Georgy's house. So much had happened that she was surprised Georgy didn't know more. "Yes, we had our talk."

"I couldn't keep Jenny here after she discovered you'd gone. Said she had too much to do. I hope it didn't cause you any problems."

"No. No problem." She'd like to tell Georgy about Jenny's pregnancy, but she couldn't. "I—I can't tell you anything, Georgy. I'm sorry."

"I understand. Are you hungry? Maria about has lunch ready."

"Yes, I—"

The ringing phone interrupted Susan's response.

Georgy went out into the entry hall where an extension rested on a small rosewood table. With her thoughts dominated by her coming discussion with Matt, Susan paid no attention to Georgy's conversation until she heard Georgy exclaim, "No! I don't believe it!"

A moment later she stepped back into the parlor, a big smile on her face. "That was Jenny."

"Ah. I assume she's still on Cloud Nine?"

"Maybe a hundred and nine. That's wonderful news."

"Yes," Susan agreed with heartfelt warmth. "Wonderful news."

"She's all right?"

"Yes, she's fine."

"Well, as I was saying, Maria almost has lunch ready, so—"

"I asked Matt to meet me here after he took Jenny and Fred back to their place. He'll probably be here any minute."

"Don't worry. We'll just set an extra place for him. Maria always cooks enough for Matt to join us. He's a favorite with her. I'll go—"

The phone rang again.

"I declare, I seldom get this many calls all week. Excuse me just a minute." Georgy returned to the entry hall.

Susan paced across the room, seeking arguments to convince Matt that her staying would be in Griffin's best interest.

Georgy appeared in the door again, but there was no smile this time. "That was Sam. He just wanted to tell me I won our bet."

"What did you bet on?"

"On whether you'd be staying."

Susan stared at Georgy, a feeling of betrayal filling her. "You bet I'd leave?"

"Shoot, girl, Sam and I bet on everything. Keeps life interesting. He bet you'd stay. I had no choice. But it was a bet I was hoping to lose. He ran into Kay and she told him you'd decided to leave." She crossed the room to touch Susan's arm. "Are you sure you can't stay?"

"I—I don't know, Georgy. That's what I need to talk to Matt about. I can't sign the contract, but I could stay until they find someone else."

"You don't think you could be happy living here?"

"It's already been decided," Matt said from the parlor door. "Don't makes things difficult for Dr. Kelly, Georgy."

"Who decided? That's what I want to know," Georgy replied, glaring at her nephew. "Me and Jenny should've handled things, instead of leaving it up to you men."

Surprisingly to Susan, Matt chuckled. "You're probably right, Aunty, dear, but what's done is done."

"Humph! Are you hungry? We're having lunch now," Georgy said, linking her arm with Susan and leading her guest to the dining room.

"I guess I could eat a little, if Dr. Kelly doesn't mind postponing our talk until after lunch." He looked at her, leaving the decision up to her.

"I think lunch is a good idea," Susan agreed. She'd heard men were more agreeable after a good meal. And it would give her time to marshal her arguments to convince the handsome mayor she should remain in Griffin.

When lunch was over, Matt escorted Susan to the parlor. Georgy left them in the entry hall with a few pungent comments on the mistake her nephew was making if he let Susan get away.

"Sorry about Georgy. She wouldn't keep on if she understood the circumstances. I assume you didn't tell her?" he asked, watching Susan as she wandered around the room.

"No. I couldn't. My father—Mr. Slater didn't want anyone to know, remember?"

"Yeah." He remembered. He remembered the heartbreak on her face when Fred made it clear he wanted her to leave. Fred's decision was understandable, but Matt vowed he'd never put himself in the position of having to deny *his* child when he had one. "Fred didn't mean to be so hard on you, Dr. Kelly. He's a good man."

She turned away from him and her voice was cool, unemotional as she agreed. "I'm sure he is."

The urge to pull her to him, offer her comfort, was strong, and Matt stepped back, even though he wasn't close to her. When she said nothing else, he finally asked, "What did you want to talk to me about?"

She faced him, a hopeful look on her face, and he grew wary. Whatever she wanted, he was going to have a hard time saying no.

"I want to stay in Griffin until you find a doctor. On a temporary basis, no contract."

He stared at her, finding it difficult to understand what she was offering. "I don't think so. We can't afford to—"

"I'm not asking for any guarantees. I'll charge the accepted rate, and I can even pay rental for the clinic. And I'll leave whenever you find someone. With any amount of notice."

Her blue eyes were anxious as she waited for him to respond. He frantically sought a way to refuse her generous offer. This wasn't a good idea. He just had to figure out why.

"I don't think—people might come to depend on you too much. Who knows when we'll find a doctor. And then there's Fred. He'd be uncomfortable with you here. And if he's uncomfortable, everything will be harder on Jenny." He felt like he was hitting below the belt to use Fred's problems, especially when those bright eyes dulled and looked away.

"I see." She turned away from him again.

"Dr. Kelly, it's a generous offer, and I do appreciate it on behalf of the people of Griffin. The town worked hard to prepare a good financial package. But we'll have to do some more work for a continued search, and they wouldn't see the need as long as you were here.''

With a question on her face, she moved across the room until she was facing him. ''Those things might be true, but they aren't impossible to overcome. Except maybe my—Mr. Slater's problem. But I'd promise to keep my identity secret.''

With scant inches between them, Matt could smell her perfume, the scent of a meadow of wild flowers on a summer day. Strands of black hair had escaped her French braid and framed her face. With her full lips tilted up in a small smile, Susan Kelly tempted him like no other woman ever had.

''I don't think it's a good idea,'' he muttered, looking away.

''Is there another reason?'' she asked quietly. ''One you haven't told me about? Do I not measure up in some way?''

He wished he could think of a shortcoming he could throw in her face, though she'd already been hurt enough by her father. But the only difficulty he hadn't mentioned wasn't a shortcoming on her part, but on his. He was too tempted by a woman he couldn't consider marrying.

With a sigh, he put his hands on her shoulders, his fingertips touching her skin through the crocheted top. Just for a minute, he couldn't resist succumbing to the temptation that had been driving him crazy. ''Yeah, there's a problem I haven't mentioned. Though I think maybe we're both aware of it.''

''What?''

''This.'' His mouth followed his word straight to those full, soft lips, in case she didn't understand. He'd been wanting to kiss her since she got off the plane. Swallowing her surprised gasp, he caressed her mouth, his tongue stroking her lips and then drinking deeply. His hands drew her against him as he stroked her back.

If she'd resisted him, he would've stopped at once. Maybe. But she'd didn't. Her arms stole around his neck and her fingers surged through his hair.

Her touch was like fire, hot, exciting, threatening to lose

control. The desire to have those hands run over his entire body almost had him peeling off his clothes. Some remnant of civilized behavior held him in check, barely.

When he came up for air, he stared down at her lips, throbbing from his touch, and Susan slowly lifted her lashes to stare at him. Even as he reached for her again, she suddenly broke away form him, putting some distance between their heated bodies.

"What do you mean?" she asked in a low voice, not looking at him.

"My actions weren't clear?" he asked, chuckling slightly, grateful she wasn't looking at him. His body's response to her was all too obvious.

"Just because there's an—an attraction doesn't mean we'd have to act on it."

At least she wasn't denying what was between them, though attraction seemed mighty tame for what he'd just experienced. "I'm not real good at resisting temptation."

"It takes two people to . . ."

"Tango?" he supplied, a wide grin on his face. For a doctor, she was kind of shy, he thought, noting her flaming cheeks. He wanted to warm his hands against her skin. Trying to concentrate on their conversation, he added, "I didn't notice much resistance on your part."

"So I was tempted, too," she stated, raising her chin and staring at him. "You're a handsome man, Mr. Griffin, and I'm only human."

"Yep. And right there is where our problem gets worse. With both of us tempted, and both of us only human, it wouldn't be long before we did something we'd both regret."

"Maybe you wouldn't regret it." She lifted her chin and glared at him.

Her words compelled him forward until he could wrap his arms around her again, feeling her softness against him. "I wouldn't regret making love with you, Susan," he whispered, "but that's as far as it could go. And I don't think you want to settle for that."

"What do you mean?"

"I refuse to be faced with the decision Fred had to make."

"What are you talking about?" Susan demanded, frowning, her hands resting on his chest.

Instead of answering her, he asked a question. "I don't know anything about your marriage, but why did your parents' marriage fail?"

"There were a lot of reasons."

"No. I think there was only one. He married someone with whom he had nothing in common. That's why my marriage failed. A city girl and a country boy. That describes your father and mother. It describes myself and Lindsay. And it describes us. I've already played that game once. I don't want the pain it brings."

She shoved herself out of his arms, anger on her expressive face. "So you're condemning every woman who doesn't live in the country? Maybe you were the problem, not her."

"Maybe." He tried to smile, even though the pain he'd wanted to avoid was filling him. "City girls are wonderful, exciting . . . but they don't adapt well. And my wife has to be willing to live here, with me. Remember at the reception last night? You said you wanted a man who could understand that your career came first? Who would cook his own meals? I can cook, but I want my wife by my side."

He swallowed, his throat suddenly dry, before adding, "We're not right for each other, in spite of what our bodies say. It's best that you leave."

She stared at him, reflecting his pain in her eyes. Damn, the woman got to him.

"I see."

The resignation in her voice tore at him. It would be so easy to forget the past, to assume if they wanted each other, everything would work out. But he knew better. He just had to keep reminding himself of that.

Without looking at him, she said, "If you'll make arrangements with Curtis, I'll leave as soon as possible." Her voice was husky with emotion and he wanted so badly to hold her, to touch her. But he was determined to be wiser this time.

"Right. I'll let you know as soon as I talk to him."

He turned to go but stopped when he felt her hand on his arm. "Yes?"

"I might as well say goodbye now." There was a fierce gleam in her eye that made him uneasy.

"Okay." He stuck out his hand, hoping to make their goodbyes simple and fast. She looked at his hand and smiled at him. He wished he could read her expression.

"No, Matt. You had your say. We'll say goodbye my way," she said.

He knew he was in trouble when she pressed her body against his and slid her hands around his neck. As if she'd cast a spell over him, she lured his lips ever closer to hers until they touched, and he was incapable of thinking.

Several heartbreaking minutes later, she slipped from his arms before he could protest. "Just so you won't forget this city girl," she murmured and left him standing in the parlor aching for her to return.

"Susan!" Georgy called as she pounded on the door.

Before Susan could answer, having finally fallen into a deep sleep after tossing and turning half the night, Georgy was beside her bed.

"Fred called. Jenny's bleeding. They're meeting you at the clinic."

Emergency room work trained Susan well. She'd thrown off her nightgown and was clawing for clothes in her suitcase by the time Georgy finished speaking. She'd packed before going to bed since Matt had left word with Georgy that Susan would fly out the next morning.

"Did he say how badly?" she asked.

"No. He's in a panic. Is there anything I can do?"

"I'll need some assistance. Would one of the nurses be available?"

"Maybe, but I'm willing. Could I help?"

"Yes, thanks, Georgy. If nothing else, you can keep Fred from going to pieces." She didn't know how experienced Georgy might be.

"I'll bring the car around front. Come down as soon as you're ready."

From long practice, Susan ran a brush through her hair and quickly braided it to keep it from her eyes. She'd left her hair long for that very reason. Slipping her feet into running shoes, she grabbed her medical bag and fled down the stairs.

In the car, Georgy drove the few blocks in no time. "I called Matt. He's coming, too. He'll be a good help with Fred."

Susan dismissed the groan that rose in her. She didn't need any more time with Matt after their conversation that afternoon. But she'd be busy with Jenny, she assured herself.

She and Georgy were ready when Fred carried Jenny into the clinic. He put her down on an examining table and Susan nodded to Georgy. She'd already explained that Georgy's first task would be to remove Fred.

Georgy grabbed his arm and pulled him out of the room. Susan ignored his protests and turned to Jenny.

"Am I going to lose the baby?" Jenny asked, panic and fear filling her words.

"I don't know, Jenny, until I've examined you. But you'll help me if you can relax. I'm going to do everything I can to save it." She smiled at her patient, hiding her own fears as best as she could.

Georgy slipped back into the room, and Susan shot her a questioning look. "Matt got here. He's taking care of Fred."

In spite of not wanting to see Matt again, Susan admitted his presence would help. Now she could concentrate on her patient.

\* \* \*

Fred paced back and forth across the waiting room. "She rested this afternoon, just like Susan said. What went wrong?"

Matt sat with his hands folded between his legs, his elbows resting on his knees. He had no answers for Fred. He could only hope and pray Susan could save the baby. And he could feel guilty for sending her away.

"She was so excited. I tried to calm her down, but—but I was excited, too. She rushed around, trying to plan the baby's room in one day. She wanted me to move furniture. Once she even grabbed—damn! Maybe that caused the bleeding. I told her not to—"

"Fred, quit trying to figure out what went wrong. We won't know anything until Susan's finished."

Fred paced in silence for five minutes before stopping in front of Matt. "It's ironic, isn't it?"

"What?"

"My first child trying to save my second one. I bet that's one for the record book."

"Yeah."

"Good thing Susan was still here."

"Yeah." And he was sending her away, he reminded himself again. He could've let her stay temporarily. What if Jenny had started bleeding tomorrow night, after Susan left. Could she have made it to San Angelo, an hour's ride away, without losing the baby?

Fred paced and Matt questioned his decision. He finally admitted that Susan was right. His objections weren't insurmountable. His real reason was personal. He was afraid of what he'd felt for her. And those kisses they'd shared, particularly the second one, hadn't lessened his fears.

But he had sworn, as mayor of Griffin, to do what was best for his town. He rubbed his face, feeling the stubble of beard. He'd made a mistake. He was going to have to ask Susan to stay until they found another doctor.

If she agreed, he'd just have to keep his distance from her. A lot of distance.

The door opened and both men rushed forward.

Susan looked at them and then nodded. "Jenny and the baby are okay . . . right now. I want to keep her here for a couple of days."

"Why? What's wrong?" Fred demanded harshly.

"The early months of pregnancy are the most dangerous. I think Jenny got overly excited, but I want to be sure the baby is stable before I let her go home."

"Okay, we'll stay," Fred said with a sigh.

Susan looked at Matt and then turned her attention back to Fred Slater. "Mr. Slater, Jenny is staying. You are not."

"But—"

"I'll let you see her. In fact, I'll let you move her to one of the beds in the clinic. But then I want you to go home. In the morning, Jenny will want you to bring her some things, and you can visit her for an hour. That's all."

"I want to be with her!" he protested.

Susan looked at Matt again, and he took Fred's arm. "Fred, she's the doctor. I think we'd better follow directions. Besides, you know how Jenny is. If you're worried, she'll try to reassure you, which will only exhaust her more."

With a quiet sigh, Fred agreed and stepped past her.

"Thank you," she murmured to Matt.

He was trying to decide how to ask her to stay when she said, in firm, doctor tones, "By the way, cancel my flight. I'm staying." Without waiting for his agreement, she turned and followed Fred into the examining room.

Matt stood frozen to the floor. She was staying, whether he wanted her to or not. He almost objected on principal. After all, he was the mayor. But she was doing exactly what he'd intended to ask her to do.

She was staying.

And he'd just have to figure out a way to keep his distance.

He followed her into the examining room.

# *Chapter Seven*

Susan convinced everyone to go home to their own beds, except for her and Jenny. Matt's exit line, promising her they would talk in the morning, however, left her unsettled.

Georgy arrived early the next morning with breakfast. Susan let Jenny sleep until her husband arrived.

"How long will you keep Jenny here?" Georgy asked as Susan moved to the receptionist's desk and looked up the number to call one of the nurses to duty.

"Probably only a couple of days. But I intend to stay in Griffin until a new doctor is found. I'm not going to leave Jenny without medical care." She pressed her lips firmly together, girding herself for battle.

Georgy's eyes widened and then a pleased smile broke across her face. "The saints be praised! Welcome to Griffin, Dr. Kelly."

With a relieved laugh, Susan dialed the nurse's number. There were no battles here. She could relax until Matt arrived.

As soon as she hung up the phone, Georgy asked if she could use it. "I've got to call Sam and tell him our bet's a draw.

That way we both win.'' With another big smile, Georgy added, ''And Griffin is the biggest winner of all.''

At nine, both Fred and Matt arrived at the clinic. Susan, when she saw the two vehicles pull into the parking lot from the waiting room window, asked Georgy to stall the two men until she checked on her patient.

Jenny woke slowly when Susan called her name. After checking her pulse and blood pressure, Susan assisted her patient into the bathroom to prepare for visitors. Once she'd tucked her back in bed, she returned to the waiting room.

''Good morning, Mr. Slater. Your wife is doing fine. Just be sure to keep her calm and resting. If you'd like, you can ensure that she eats her breakfast.''

''Thanks.'' He had leaped to his feet as soon as Susan entered. Georgy handed him the tray prepared for Jenny, and Susan led the way to his wife's bed.

When she returned to the waiting room, Leslie, the second nurse, was waiting. Susan gave her instructions and, after she left, turned to the one person who might disturb her arrangements.

''Good morning, Matt.''

''Dr. Kelly.''

She noted his formal address. ''Perhaps I should have addressed you as mayor.''

''What's the matter with you, Matt?'' Georgy wanted to know. ''Why are you being so all-fired stiff-necked?''

Susan almost laughed aloud as his cheeks flushed in embarrassment. It did her good to hear Georgy take the all-mighty, too-handsome mayor down a peg or two.

''I thought I should show some respect here in her office,'' Matt insisted, irritation in his voice.

''Thank you,'' Susan murmured, though she wasn't sure she believed him.

''Ah, then you're willing for her to stay? Even if she's only here temporarily, I think it'll be wonderful for the town.'' Georgy's endorsement was enthusiastic.

"Yes."

Susan's eyes widened and she stared at Matt. "Yes, what?"

"Yes, your staying temporarily will be wonderful for the town." He nodded as he finished his admission and Susan felt the tension melt.

He wasn't going to fight her. She could stay. Just until they found a new doctor, of course. Unable to hold back a smile, she took a step toward Matt. "Thank you—"

She stopped as he backed away, as if she had a communicable disease. Stiffening, she repeated without the smile, "Thank you for agreeing to let me stay."

Georgy stood there, staring at first one and then the other of them. "What's the matter with you two? You'd think you were attending your best friend's funeral."

Breaking her gaze from Matt's solemn face, Susan tried to reassure Georgy. "We're both trying to consider all the aspects of our decision, Georgy. For example, I'll need a place to live. Would you consider letting me stay with you, as a boarder?"

Successfully distracted, Georgy enthusiastically agreed to Susan's request. She even offered to call the phone company that very day to have a separate line installed for Susan so late night calls wouldn't wake Georgy.

As soon as she hurried from the room, intent on doing everything she could to install Susan comfortably in Griffin, silence fell.

Matt cleared his throat. "You understand that we can't offer you anything extra since we still have to find a permanent doctor."

"My father may not have told you, but I'm financially independent. Money isn't an issue."

His gaze sharpened. "Then why did you want to know about Fred's situation?"

That was a question she'd prefer not to answer. She fought to keep the blood from her cheeks. "Curiosity about my father."

Even as she said that last word, she looked around her, afraid someone might have overheard.

Matt, too, recognized the difficulty. "You must be careful. Do I have your word that you won't reveal that particular piece of information to anyone?"

She stiffened, formality returning to her words. "Of course."

"I haven't talked to Fred, yet, but I imagine he'll be happy for you to stay. His first concern is for Jenny and the baby."

His words hurt, but they weren't anything Susan hadn't recognized herself. She turned away, hoping to hide the pain. "Of course," she repeated.

She must not have been completely successful because Matt moved to her side and touched her arm. "I didn't mean to hurt you, Susan."

Swallowing the knot in her throat, Susan could only shake her head. Speaking was impossible at the moment. His arms pulled her into his warmth, and she couldn't resist laying her head on his shoulder.

"Well, well, well," Sam's dry voice interrupted their privacy, and both of them jumped back from each other.

"Looks like everything's goin' well," the sheriff said, then chuckled.

"That's enough, Sam. I was just—just helping the doctor."

"Yes, sir, Mayor," Sam said in mock obedience while a sly grin spread across his face. "I reckon you'll have a lot of volunteers if that's the job description."

Susan wished her skin wasn't so pale, making a blush glow like a neon light. As Matt ground his teeth in frustration, she tried to change the subject. "Did you need something, Sheriff?"

"Well, yes and no. I didn't, but some folks called the office wantin' to know if you'd see patients."

"No," Matt answered.

"Yes," Susan responded.

"Which will it be?" Sam pressed, staring at the two of them.

"The answer is yes," Susan said calmly, but she dared Matt with her gaze to contradict her. "I'm going to be Griffin's doctor until a permanent one is found. Be sure you tell everyone that I'm only temporary, Sam."

"Yeah, be sure to tell everyone that," Matt growled.

"Might testy this morning, aren't you, Matt?" Sam demanded, staring at the mayor. "Didn't you get enough sleep last night?"

"No, I didn't. I came into town to help with Fred."

"What happened to Fred?" Sam lost all the teasing from his voice as concern for a friend filled it.

"Mr. Slater is fine," Susan assured him. "Jenny is my patient, and I can't tell you more than that. You can ask Mr. Slater about it later. He's in with Jenny right now."

"Jenny's sick? What's wrong with her?"

"Sam, I just told you to ask her husband. I can't reveal anything. I'm her doctor."

"Humph! Seems to me the sheriff ought to be kept informed about these things," he protested, scowling at Susan.

"Sam thinks, as sheriff, he should be privy to all the gossip in town," Matt advised her wryly.

"Not gossip!" Sam contradicted him. "But it helps if I know what's going on."

"I'm sure it does," Susan said, trying to soothe him, "but you'll have to get this news from the source."

"I'll do that. When are you goin' to be open for customers?" Sam asked, switching subjects.

The clinic had been set up with an office for her and examining rooms that could be used for out-patients as well as those staying in the clinic. "Well, I'm here this morning, so I can see anyone who needs me, I guess. I'll have to think about what kind of regular hours I want to keep." She really hadn't considered that aspect of her decision just yet.

"Let me know when you have. I'll pass the word around." Sam stood there, his hands on his hips, seemingly unwilling to leave.

"Is there anything else, Sam?"

"Well, I wondered if I might say hello to Jenny. We're good friends, you know."

Susan grinned. The sheriff couldn't stand out knowing what

was going on in his town. "If you promise to only stay a minute and not upset her."

He nodded and crossed the Waiting Room to enter the clinic, leaving Matt and Susan alone again.

Matt, too, seemed reluctant to leave. Susan wondered if he had something else to tell her. "Matt? Do we need to make any kind of formal agreement?"

"Yeah, probably. I'll get our city attorney to draw up something. You're sure you want to stay?"

"Yes, I want to stay. I don't have any choice, considering— considering the circumstances. Since I don't have to open up a practice at once to pay off school loans, I can please myself. And staying here pleases me."

"Temporarily."

"Why do you keep saying that word, as if I might forget?" His insistence that she would be leaving, hurt her almost as much as her father's rejection.

"I'm not reminding you," he explain in low tones, his gaze boring into her. "I'm reminding myself." He drew closer to her again. "What happened yesterday mustn't happen again."

She wouldn't look away, or let him see how much she wanted to touch him. Keeping her gaze cool, she tried to be nonchalant. "You mean the kisses?"

"Yeah. The kisses." He moved a step closer.

"You started it." She nibbled on her bottom lip, thinking she sounded as mature as a second grader on the school playground.

"Yeah. And that's why I need to keep reminding myself that you're leaving."

Her chin came up. "I won't let you forget."

He moved another step closer, his body almost touching hers, his masculine scent wrapping around her, and reached out to trace her jawline with one finger. "Even knowing that you're leaving won't stop me from wanting you."

She clamped her teeth down on her bottom lip to keep it from trembling and said nothing. She couldn't.

"If you should decide," he whispered, his mouth coming

ever so much closer to hers, "that wanting would be enough, let me know."

Closing her eyes, she shook her head no and prayed he'd go away. He was tempting her as she'd never been tempted, and he knew it.

"Susan?"

"No. It wouldn't be enough," she whispered, opening her eyes to stare up at him. "It wouldn't be enough," she repeated.

"No, I guess it wouldn't." He jerked away from her and strode to the door before stopping. "If you need anything, let me know. Otherwise, I'll keep my distance."

He looked at her one last time, and she fought the urge to run to him, to take whatever he offered and hope for the best. But she didn't. She already had one failed marriage as a warning to her, in addition to her parents's marriage. Matt was right. Why look for pain?

"Bye, Susan," he muttered. Before she could say goodbye, he was gone. She'd never felt so lonely, not even when her mother died.

"Well, I know the secret now, Susan," Sam boomed as he stepped through the door. "And that's real good news."

She jumped and then composed her features before she turned to look at the sheriff. "Yes, it is, isn't it?"

"Glad you were here. And Georgy says you'll be stayin' until we find a permanent doctor."

"Yes, that's right. I couldn't leave Jenny on her own."

"Why can't you just stay? Seems to me you like us well enough." Sam's sharp gaze watched her, waiting for an answer.

"I'm afraid my reasons are personal, Sam, but you're right. I do like Griffin and the people, very much. So, I'm going to stay temporarily. That's the most I can do."

"Humph! If we knew what those reasons were, we could work on them, maybe help you change your mind." Sam never seemed to give up on something.

Susan sighed. Crossing the room, she stopped beside the older man and kissed his cheek. "You're a dear, but that's all

I can tell you. Now, I've got to check on my patient and chase away her husband. She needs her rest.''

Susan entered Jenny's room to find Fred sitting on the side of the bed, both arms around Jenny. The two of them were talking quietly, following Susan's strict orders to remain calm.

"Mr. Slater, I'm afraid it's time for Jenny to rest now. If you'd like to come visit her again this evening, at suppertime, I think I can persuade Maria to cook dinner for both of you."

"Oh, that would be nice, Susan," Jenny answered at once. "But I'd rather Fred stayed."

"If I'm going to be your doctor, Jenny Slater," Susan added, watching her father carefully, "then I expect you to follow orders."

"Are you? Are you going to be my doctor?" Jenny asked, her eyes lighting up with happiness.

"I've agreed to stay until they find a permanent doctor. I don't want you to be without medical care." Looking at her father's worried frown, she repeated, "But it's only temporary."

Like Sam, Jenny wanted to argue. "But if you're willing to stay a little while, maybe you'll decide you like it here."

"We'll just take everything one day at a time, Jenny. And right now, our main concern is making sure you and junior stay healthy. So, it's time for your husband to go home and do some work, and for you to take a nap." She nodded to Fred who reluctantly moved off the bed.

He leaned down and kissed his wife goodbye. As he moved toward the door, Susan followed him. "The nurse will be in to take your blood pressure and temperature before you go to sleep, Jenny."

When she and her father were both in the Waiting Room, Jenny spoke again. "Mr. Slater."

He turned and waited for her to continue.

"I just wanted to—to reassure you that our discussion yesterday is forgotten. I'm staying because of Jenny. I hope it won't upset you."

He didn't answer at once. Susan watched the struggle on his features, a mixture of fear, concern and pain. Her teeth sank into her bottom lip, but she remained silent. She'd said all she needed to say.

"I wasn't afraid you'd tell anyone, Susan. I'm sorry about—about everything. And I'm grateful that you'll be here for Jenny. Last night I thought—I was afraid—"

"She's going to be just fine . . . if she follows orders." She nodded, trying to hide the moisture in her eyes. "They're both going to be just fine."

"Thank you."

He turned to go, and Susan did nothing to hold him. She had said her piece and received agreement if not approval. It was all she could ask for.

As he put his hand on the doorknob, he stopped and bowed his head. Susan watched him, wondering why he wasn't leaving.

"Susan?"

"Yes?"

"It probably doesn't mean anything to you, but—but I'm proud of you." He hurried through the door, not waiting for her reaction to his words.

Susan stood alone in the waiting room, tears streaming down her pale cheeks.

# Chapter Eight

Susan was amazed at how well she settled into life in Griffin. After the weekend, she set regular hours for patients, but she left Wednesday and a couple of afternoons free, except for emergencies.

Jenny went home on Monday morning. Both she and Fred promised to follow orders faithfully. They also assured her they would call if Jenny even felt a twinge of discomfort.

Susan smiled. They might be older than most first parents, but they were just as nervous. She discovered there were four other pregnant women among her new patients.

"Has anyone ever attended birth classes here in Griffin?" she asked Georgy at breakfast Wednesday morning.

"Birth classes? I guess not. I've never heard of any. What do you need those for if you've got a doctor or a midwife?"

"They help prepare the new parents for what really happens. It makes the mother and father less nervous."

"Well, I reckon you'd better have some of those classes or Fred Slater will have a nervous breakdown long before that baby gets born."

Both women laughed before Susan continued, "I want to talk to you about some other projects, too." She briefly outlined several classes she'd like to start about teenage pregnancy, drug abuse and parenting.

"Those are good ideas," Georgy said, "but a little ambitious. I mean, we just got you here."

"I know," Susan agreed with a sigh. "My professors always warned me I tried to go too fast."

"Well, we'll have Matt to supper tonight and talk about everything."

"No! I mean, I probably will need to, uh, visit—"

"Wait just a minute. You can't work around the clock. You've already put in extra hours at the clinic these past two days. Don't push yourself so hard."

"Okay," Susan agreed. "But don't ask Matt to come for my benefit."

"Why not?"

Susan played with her fork, stirring the scrambled eggs around the plate. Finally, she mumbled, "Because I don't think he'd come."

The past two days, she'd looked for him. Everytime a door opened, she'd think it might be him. After all, he was responsible for her being here. She had thought perhaps he'd check up on her.

"Why not?" Georgy asked again, watching her closely, interest in her golden eyes, so much like Matt's. Her intentions were obvious. But Susan knew, as Georgy seemed not to, that her plan to matchmake between Susan and her nephew would never work.

"Georgy, I've been married before and it wasn't a happy experience. And Matt's first marriage seems to have convinced him that no one from different backgrounds can have a good marriage."

"You mean he's comparing you and that piece of baggage he married?" Georgy demanded, outraged.

Susan couldn't hold back her smile when she heard Georgy's opinion of the former Mrs. Griffin. "I'm afraid so."

"Men are so ridiculous! I'll have a talk with him."

"Georgy, please, don't. Let's let everything settle down first."

Sighing, Georgy nodded in agreement. "You're right."

Susan's heart beat slowed, grateful that Georgy wasn't going to pursue her matchmaking idea. Susan had enough trouble resisting Matt without any pressure from Georgy.

"Thank you for calling, Mrs. Jacoby. Yes, I agree. I'll certainly tell her." Matt hung up the phone with a big sigh.

"Another one?" his housekeeper, Ethel, asked.

"Yeah. That woman's been doctor here for less than a week, and everyone loves her. If I get one more call telling me how wonderful she is, I'll—"

The phone rang again.

Ethel set a plate of food on the table. "You sit down and eat. I'll get the phone."

Matt wasn't about to turn down that offer. Every minute he'd spent in the house, he'd had to listen to praise of the one woman he wanted to forget. Susan Kelly had won the hearts of the townspeople with her doctoring. She'd won his heart— no, not heart, he hurriedly amended. She'd attracted him with her beauty, her determination. Her kisses hadn't hurt either.

Damn. He'd promised himself he wouldn't think about his lips touching hers. He'd almost hammered his thumb off earlier when he'd let his thoughts return to Susan.

"That was Georgy," Ethel reported as she returned to the table. "She was disappointed you were already eating. She wanted you to come to dinner."

"I'm glad I had to eat early," he muttered, not looking up.

"Well, she wanted to know if you could come over and discuss some ideas that doctor has, but I reminded her it was

Wednesday and you had the Cattlemen's Association meeting tonight.''

"Thanks, Ethel. I appreciate you taking care of that. I'll check in with her tomorrow." While Susan's busy at the clinic. He didn't want any tête-à-têtes with the beautiful doctor.

Even though he hadn't left the ranch since he went to church on Sunday, he hadn't been able to avoid news of Susan. It seemed as if the town was conspiring to remind him constantly of her presence.

He didn't know why she was working so hard to win over the town. After her assurance of financial independence, he'd asked Fred about her situation. According to her father, Susan's words had been an understatement. She wasn't just independent. She could buy Griffin, Texas, lock, stock and barrel, and still have money left over.

So why was she out busting her butt, tending every little scrape, and half the time not even charging her patients? Once word got out that she was a soft touch, she'd be flooded with malingerers.

"Did you say something?" Ethel asked, sitting down across from him. In her fifties, she'd worked for his parents after she married one of their cowboys. Her children were grown now, her husband dead, and she was content as his housekeeper. He couldn't imagine the place without her.

"No, nothing."

"Well, it really wasn't a word. Kind of a growl."

"I was just thinking about a problem."

Because Susan Kelly's wealth was another problem.

In spite of what he told himself about he and Susan having nothing in common, he knew the attraction he felt was wearing down his cynicism.

But a woman who was wealthy wouldn't want to live in Griffin. She couldn't even spend much here. There just weren't enough stores. Though his ex-wife had tried.

Lindsay'd had the opposite problem. Her major in college had been finding a wealthy husband. He hadn't realized he'd been chosen based on his bank account until it was too late. She'd found someone with money, though nothing to compare to Susan's, but she hadn't wanted to live in a small, isolated town. The price was too high.

"You'd better grab your hat and be on your way, or you're going to be late," Ethel reminded him, interrupting his thoughts.

"Right. Thanks, Ethel," he said as he stood. Thanks for reminding him of his meeting, and thanks for giving him something else to think about. He'd spent more than enough time on Susan Kelly, especially since he'd set out to forget her.


"What a brave guy you were, Peter," Susan said with a smile. She patted her miniature patient on the shoulder and then lifted him down from the examining table. "Kay has a surprise for you."

She'd sent the nurse over to the general store on her first day to find small toys for the children as rewards for good behavior. As Peter picked out his toy, she conferred with his mother, reviewing the care she'd given the boy.

After Peter and his mother left, she and Kay exchanged sighs. Though they'd had Wednesday off, they'd had a full load of patients today.

"Were they the last?" she asked her nurse.

"Yes," Kay assured her with a grin. "I didn't know Griffin had so many sick folks."

"They're just trying to catch up on everything at once. We've given a lot of injections that won't be repeated for several years, at least. Things will slow down soon."

"I hope so."

"Do you want Denise to come help you straighten up?" Susan had hired a high school student to work as receptionist until school started.

"That's a good idea."

As Kay turned to head for the Waiting Room, Susan stopped

her. "Stay here. I'll get her, and then I'm going to my office to finish up the charts."

The waiting room wasn't as pristine as it had been that first day, but Susan didn't worry. It was being put to good use, and that was what mattered. She asked Denise to help the nurse, and they were both turning to go back through the swinging door when the outer door opened.

"I'll tell them we're closed," Denise said.

"Doc!" A dusty cowboy, his hat pulled down low on his head, looked relieved when he recognized Susan.

"I'll take care of this, Denise. He doesn't look too sick," Susan said, a smile on her face, sending the youngster on her way.

"Oh, it's not me. It's the boss."

"What's wrong?" Susan asked, moving to the man's side.

"We think maybe his arm is broken. This two-by-four slipped and hit him and—"

"Where is he?"

"Pony's bringin' him in."

Susan felt thoroughly confused now. A man who looked like a cowboy appeared to be a carpenter and said an animal was bringing in the injured man. She peered over his shoulder out the door he held open.

"Oh, dear," she muttered beneath her breath.

"It don't look that bad, does it?" the cowboy asked, looking worried.

Susan automatically slipped back into the role of doctor, reassuring him. "No, of course not. I was just surprised at the identity of the Boss.

"Oh. Come on in, Pony." He pushed the door wider and the big man apparently named Pony assisted the boss, Matt Griffin, into the waiting room. The broken arm was wrapped in a homemade sling and hung limply.

"We'll have to take x-rays. Can you help him into the examining room?" She was grateful the clinic had a small, portable x-ray machine.

Both men assisted their employer into the examining room.

"We was building the new barn and a piece of lumber slipped and fell on him," Pony explained as they eased their "Boss" onto the examining table.

"I'll call my nurse," Susan said, slipping from the room.

Kay immediately dropped what she was doing and pushed in the x-ray machine. The two cowboys stepped out to the Waiting Room and she and Kay made pictures of the broken arm in only minutes.

Matt hadn't spoken since he'd come in. By the grimace on his face that intensified as they'd moved his arm for the x-rays, he was in a lot of discomfort.

"Are you all right, Matt?" she asked softly. "I can give you something to ease the pain."

"No," he grunted, avoiding looking at her.

Somehow, she'd expected that response. "Kay, the x-rays won't be ready for a few minutes. I'll keep an eye on Matt, and you can finish up in the other room."

When they were alone, she crossed over to the sink and wet a paper towel with cool water. Returning to her patient's side, she said calmly, "I'm going to clean you up a little while we're waiting."

His blond hair was dark with sweat and well sanded with sawdust, which also covered his sweaty skin. She ran her fingers through his hair, shaking the sawdust out, then wiped his face with the cool towel.

"This isn't necessary," he growled at her.

She couldn't hide her smile. For once, she had the upper hand with Matt Griffin. "Doctors always insist on their patients being clean. It's a rule." She reached for the top button on his shirt.

"What are you doing?"

Arching one eyebrow, she murmured, "I'm going to have my way with you, of course." When he didn't even crack a smile, she shrugged and tried another answer. "I'm taking off your shirt. It will have to come off before I can treat your arm.''

''Shouldn't the nurse be doing this?'' he asked, frowning darkly.

''Normally, yes, but she's doing some other things. Besides, I'm not a hoity-toity doctor who wants a nurse to do everything for her.''

He didn't offer any more protests, and Susan continued unbuttoning his shirt. When she pulled it open to ease it off his shoulders, she paused briefly, admiring the man. She'd suspected he was in good shape, but properly dressed, there was no way she could've guessed how impressive a specimen of manhood he was.

''Are you going to undress me or not?'' he demanded impatiently.

Hoping her cheeks weren't too red, Susan immediately slid the shirt off his good arm. Then she concentrated on moving his injured arm as little as possible. After the shirt was removed, she returned to the sink. Rewetting the paper towel, she moved to his side again and rubbed it across his chest, scarcely breathing, to dislodge the sawdust that clung to the silky blond curls that spiraled down to his jeans.

*You're not being professional, Susan. You're supposed to treat the patient, not become turned on by his bare chest.* She retreated from him and then turned her back, trying to get control of her outrageous response to Matt Griffin.

''Finished?'' he drawled, making it clear to Susan that he knew exactly what was happening.

Keeping her back to him, she returned to the sink to wash her hands. ''Yes, I am. I hope you're more comfortable now.''

''My jeans are a little tight.''

Startled by his response, she jerked around to stare at him wide-eyed. It took all her will power not to see if his words were accurate.

''I don't think—''

''Come here.''

Not moving, she asked carefully, "What do you want?"

"My pound of flesh."

"I don't understand."

"Come here."

As if mesmerized by his golden eyes, Susan crossed back to stand in front of him. "Yes?"

"My turn," he muttered and reached out with his good arm to pull her off-balance against him, his lips descending to hers for an all-out assault on her senses.

Susan lost all sense of time or place, her whole being enveloped in Matt's embrace. How long they would have continued their enjoyment of each other she didn't know, but a deep moan, of pain not arousal, brought her back to reality.

Pulling away, she questioned breathlessly, "Your arm? Did you move your arm?"

"I don't know," he muttered, leaning toward her, his lips seeking hers.

"Matt, we've got to stop. Kay will be in any minute with your x-rays." Now that she'd awakened from his seductive touch, she was determined not to fall under his spell again.

She moved to the sink to rinse her hot cheeks with cold water.

"Come back," Matt urged.

"No."

He tried to slide off the end of the table and jostled his arm again. His barely contained groan had her rushing back to his side, but he was in no state to take advantage of her nearness.

Kay came through the door just as Susan was easing Matt's arm back against his body. "Here are the x-rays, Doctor." She hung them against the lighted screen and the two of them looked at the pictures together.

"About what I expected," Susan said, breathing deeply to slow her erratic heart beat.

"How bad is it?" Matt demanded.

"A simple fracture. No permanent damage. We'll just have to put you in a cast. In six weeks, you'll be good as new."

She eased the sling off his shoulder and examined his bare arm. "I think we'd better wait until tomorrow to put the cast on, though, since it's swollen."

"Shall I prepare a bed for him?" Kay asked.

"Yes, but first bring me a temporary brace. Then put him in one of the semi-private rooms so I can keep an eye on him and still get some rest." Susan didn't look up from Matt's arm until she realized Kay was still standing beside her. With a frown, she looked at her nurse. "Yes, Kay?"

"Um, Doctor, I don't think—that is, he's a man."

Stunned by what the woman was implying, and feeling slightly guilty because of what had just happened, Susan snapped, "So?"

"I mean, people might talk."

"Just do as I asked," Susan ordered stiffly, seething inside that Kay, or any of the townspeople, would think she might behave so unprofessionally. Then, memory of what had just occurred in her examining room made her feel even worse.

"Yes, Doctor," Kay muttered and fled from the room.

"Thanks, Matt," Susan muttered, knowing she was being unfair but beyond caring about the man's sensibilities. "This is all your fault!"

"My fault? Doctor, I don't know what you're talking about." His golden eyes sparkled with mock innocence.

"Yes, you do. If I hadn't felt so guilty about what just happened in here, I wouldn't have snapped at Kay. You stay put. I need to go apologize to her."

# *Chapter Nine*

Matt watched Susan stomp from the room, still able to appreciate the gentle swing of her hips in the navy slacks she wore. He'd better get his mind on something distracting, like a tornado or a blinding rain storm or a month long drought. Because he'd been right.

Having the doctor examine him with her long, slender fingers, touching his heated skin, standing near him, had been more than he could take. The kiss had been inevitable from the moment she'd touched him. Even the pain in his arm wasn't enough to distract him from the desire Dr. Susan Kelly could summon at a second's notice.

He hoped Kay won the argument about Susan sharing a room with him tonight. He'd never get any sleep.

"Susan?"

Georgy's voice would've summoned the dead at that pitch. Matt knew why she was there, anyway. Word got around fast in Griffin.

"In here, Georgy."

She burst into the room, anxiety on her features.

"Matt! I just heard. Are you all right? Where's Susan?"

Before he could answer any of her questions, Susan joined them. "I'm right here. And Matt broke his arm. He'll be fine."

"Oh, you poor boy. How did it happen? Why isn't his arm in a cast?" When Georgy got upset, words just poured forth with little let-up.

"Georgy, calm down. Susan's taking good care of me." He shot a look over Georgy's shoulder to tweak Susan's memory of the most interesting care he'd received.

In spite of her red cheeks, she spoke calmly. "I haven't put a cast on because his arm is swollen. I want to wait until the swelling goes down. We're going to stablize the break with this temporary brace," she explained. She eased his arm into the brace she'd brought back with her, using the velcro fasteners to hold it in place. "After the swelling goes away, then we'll put on a cast."

"When will that be? In an hour or two?"

"No, Georgy, it won't be that soon. I'm going to keep him here overnight." Susan picked up his chart and made a notation in it.

"Overnight? I'll stay with him." Georgy reached out to comfort Matt, but she picked the wrong arm to pat.

"Ouch! Damn it, Georgy, that's the broken one."

"Oh, I'm so sorry. I don't know what I'm doing. It's just so upsetting, you being in the hospital. I promised your Mama I'd take good care of you and—" she stopped talking and burst into tears, covering her face with her hands.

"Aw, Georgy, I didn't mean to yell at you," Matt hurriedly said, his voice softening.

His apology seemed unacceptable to Susan as she threw her arms around his aunt. "Now, Georgy, you know I wouldn't lie to you. Matt's going to be just fine. He's grumpy," she added, glaring at him, "but that's nothing unusual. Don't worry about him."

"I don't mean to go to pieces on you," Georgy apologized, sniffing between words. "Usually, I'm strong as a horse. But

Matt's my only family, you know. He's the boy I never had. I just—''

"It's okay, Georgy, I understand.''

Matt watched the two women, a wry grin on his face. He was forgotten as one consoled the other. Georgy was a tower of strength when solving other people's problems. But the few times he'd been hurt, she'd fallen to pieces. He should've expected it.

What about Susan? If she was attracted to him, would she be able to treat him? Did doctors do that sort of thing? Of course, she'd had difficulty remaining calm when she was wiping off his chest.

If their positions were reversed, he—the sudden image of his removing Susan's shirt wiped all coherent thought from his head.

"What are you thinking about?'' Susan demanded sternly, standing in front of Georgy, staring at him, her hands cocked on her hips.

His gaze flew involuntarily to her chest and then to her face. Her cheeks were flaming, making her all the more enticing. He tried to wipe all emotion from his face, but he suspected he was unsuccessful.

"Nothing,'' he assured her.

"We need to get you horizontal so we can prop up your arm. The longer you sit with it hanging down, the more it will swell.''

The word horizontal and Susan in the same context didn't make it any easier for Matt to think of less enticing things, like poison ivy, an abcessed tooth, his broken arm. As hard as he tried, he couldn't hold back a silly grin.

"What's wrong with you, Matt?'' Susan demanded, frowning at him.

"It's the pain,'' Georgy assured her. "Have you given him anything for the pain?''

"No, he refused. I think it would be best to get him settled in bed before I do that.''

"That's probably a good idea. If he fell, he'd be too heavy for us to lift," Georgy agreed.

"I'm not going to—"

"Susan?" a deep voice called from the waiting room.

"That's Sam," Georgy hurriedly said before calling, "In here, Sam."

Only seconds later, the sheriff burst into the room, a frown on his face. "What's going on here? What happened, boy?"

"I suppose she called you?" Matt asked grumpily, not enjoying all the fuss. "I swear, I don't know why you two haven't gotten married. You might as well since you tell each other everything."

There was an awkward silence that pierced his frustration and pain. He looked at his beloved aunt and discovered she'd turned a bright red and was glaring at him. Sam was almost as red, but he was staring everywhere but at Georgy or Matt.

"You sure know how to make people feel appreciated for showing you concern, cowboy," Susan drawled.

Before he could protest or apologize, and he wasn't sure which would be appropriate, she turned to Sam.

"Since you're here, Sam, would you mind helping this grouch to bed? He'd probably appreciate some assistance from a man."

"Sure, Susan. Be happy to." Sam still refused to look at him, and Matt felt about as low as he could get. Sam had been his friend ever since he could remember.

"Georgy," Susan continued even as she stepped back from Matt's side, "do you think Maria could fix dinner for both Matt and me? I know it's extra trouble for you to bring it over, but I'd really appreciate it. And then, I might get you to stay a few minutes with Matt while I go home and shower and change. I'm feeling sticky after the day I've put in."

"Why, of course I will," Georgy agreed, looking a little less embarrassed.

"Let's send these two on their way, and then we'll discuss

the menu for our patient. Thought you may want to put him on bread and water. It might improve his manners.''

"Georgy,'' Matt began as Sam took his good arm to help him off the table, ''I didn't mean to—to upset either one of you.''

"Matt, you've talked enough. Just go with Sam. You'll see Georgy later,'' Susan ordered sternly.

Growing crosser by the moment, resenting being treated like a kindergartner, Matt nevertheless obeyed Susan's command. He'd made a mess of everything. As soon as he and Sam were alone, he'd apologize.

"Easy, son,'' Sam cautioned as he tried to hurry from the room.

When the door closed behind them, Matt stopped. "Sam, I owe you an apology. I know you and Georgy are just friends. I shouldn't have said that.''

"Don't bother me none,'' Sam assured him, a wry smile on his face. "It's Georgy who's embarrassed. I'm not good enough for Georgy Griffin, and everyone knows it.''

Matt had started forward again when Sam's words pierced his head. "What are you talking about?''

Sam didn't pretend to misunderstand. "Georgy's one of the Griffins. She's a beautiful lady with an education and a lot of money. I reckon she could marry anyone she wanted to. I'm makin' it okay, but I'm never gonna be rich.''

"You think that matters to Georgy?'' Matt was almost insulted by Sam's words.

"Come on, boy. I've got to get you to bed before Susan skins me alive.'' Sam tugged on his good arm, trying to ignore Matt's question.

But Sam's response had triggered a dozen memories in Matt's head. Sam escorting Georgy to town functions, carefully opening doors for her, sharing a smile, a look, his gaze following her across the room. Acting like he couldn't tear his eyes from her. Just like Matt did with Susan.

Sam wanted Georgy. That was a mind-boggling idea. The

thought of his aunt and his friend in a passionate embrace was almost embarrassing. Until he thought about Susan at Georgy's age. Would he still want her? Hell, yes!

What should he do now?

He allowed Sam to assist him in undressing and taking care of necessities, while he mulled over what he should do next.

Once he was tucked in the bed, Kay came in and propped his arm up on a stack of pillows. Sam was edging toward the door, apparently planning on making his escape.

"Wait, Sam."

Sam swung around to stare at him and Kay did the same, startled by his command.

"Is there something you need? I'll get it for you before I leave," she offered.

"No, thanks, Kay. I'm sure your husband is waiting for you to get home. I just wanted to have a word with Sam."

"I got lots of work waitin' for me," Sam protested.

"We've got to talk, Sam."

Kay told them both goodbye and slipped away before Sam could protest.

The sheriff walked over to the window and stared out of it, his back to Matt. "Now don't go gettin' all het up over what you said earlier. I told you it don't matter."

"Sam, how long have you been a widower?"

The sheriff spun around, surprise on his face. "You know Mary Lou's been dead four years, Matt. Why'd you ask that?"

"I just wondered how stupid you've been, and now I know. About three years' worth."

Matt hoped what he was doing worked. Otherwise, he might lose a dear friend. But he figured it was worth the gamble.

"What are you saying?" Sam asked in his most threatening voice, the one he used to scare teenaged miscreants.

"Maybe I'm misjudging you. Maybe you didn't fall in love with Georgy until recently." He looked at his old friend expectantly.

Sam turned his back on him again and let out a deep sigh, his chin sinking to his chest.

"Sam?"

The sheriff turned around with the saddest face he'd ever seen. "I fell in love with your aunt when she was sixteen, the second day after we moved to Griffin. I'd never seen anyone so beautiful."

"Did you two date?"

"Of course not!"

"Why? If you felt that way, why didn't you ask her out?"

"Son, my daddy was a sharecropper, barely scrapin' together a livin'. I was eighteen, never finished high school. The army drafted me and I left Griffin for four years. That was probably the best thing that could've happened to me, 'cause I had no business even lookin' at Georgy, and I knew it."

"But you married Mary Lou."

"Sure I did. I came back here and Georgy was away at that fancy school of hers. She came home that summer, bringing some friends with her. College friends. I'm not educated, but I'm not stupid, either."

He paced across the room, his head down. "Mary Lou loved me. I told her—I told her I cared about her, but I wasn't sure that was enough. She said it was."

Matt felt like crying, watching Sam in such pain. He'd never guessed. After his mother and father died shortly after his marriage, both Sam and Georgy had been there for him. He'd done a lot of taking, but it didn't seem he'd done much giving.

"Sam, I think Georgy cares about you."

Sam straightened his shoulders, as if shaking off the past, and smiled at him. "Sure she does, son. We're friends. Always have been. She and Mary Lou were good friends and it just kind of happened, natural like."

That might be Sam's interpretation of what happened, but Matt remembered Mary Lou. She'd been a hypochondriac, always complaining about some problem. Often as not, Sam had cooked dinner for both of them after working all day. Not the kind of woman his aunt would've had much patience with. Unless she had another reason.

"Well, is our grouchy patient settled in?" Susan asked, strolling in, a smile on her face.

"I'm having a private conversation with Sam," he protested, hoping Susan would go away. He should've known better.

"He probably needs his rest," Sam hurriedly said, easing toward the door.

"And I'm sure you've had about all his company you can stand, Sam. I appreciate the help."

"No problem. I'll check on you tomorrow, son."

"Sam, wait—" He stopped because the door closed behind the sheriff.

"Damn, Susan, that was important!"

"It didn't seem important to Sam."

"Because he doesn't understand!"

"And *you're* going to enlighten him?" She made it sound like his enlightening anyone was an impossibility.

"Why are you here?" he demanded.

"Because I couldn't stay away from your charming self," she assured him and laid a cool hand across his cheek.

He jerked away from her in anger, and her eyebrows soared. Without another word, she raised the head of his bed and poured a glass of water. Then she handed him a small paper cup and the water.

"What's this?"

"Something to make you more comfortable."

"I don't want a pain pill. They make me crazy," he protested, frowning at her.

"This one is very mild. It will just relax you a little. Then maybe I can stand to be in the same room with you."

He scowled at her. "You promise it won't mess me up? I've got to talk to Georgy. Tonight."

"You'll still be able to talk to Georgy."

"And make sense?"

"As much as you ever do."

"Thanks a lot," he growled before swallowing the pill and taking a drink of water to wash it down.

She leaned over to lower his bed again. The shadow between her breasts was visible, and his breath caught.

"Is something wrong? Did I jostle your arm?" Gone was the sarcasm and teasing, replaced by a concern that warmed him and eased some of his irritation.

"No, I'm fine, but leave my bed propped up like it was. I'm not tired."

"Good, because you still have to eat dinner."

"Yeah. You like baseball?"

She looked at him, surprise on her face. "Baseball? Did you think you were going to get up a game anytime soon?"

He grinned. It didn't take long for Susan to make him forget everything but her. "Nope. But the Rangers are playing tonight, and the game's on television."

"Really? Terrific. Of course I'm a Rangers fan. After all, they play just outside of Dallas."

He enjoyed the enthusiasm in her face. "I wasn't sure a sophisticated lady like you would watch baseball. It didn't sound like it would be your grandmother's cup of tea."

"It wasn't. But my step-grandfather, James Thorne, was a fanatic. Once he even owned a small part of the Rangers. Grandmother let me go with him only because he had no children and she wanted to make sure he left his estate to her family, not remote cousins on his side."

"And did he?"

There was sadness in her eyes that told him she'd really cared about the man. "Yes, most of it. But he left *me* his love of baseball."

"I think you got the best of the deal," he agreed softly, reaching out to clasp her hand.

Georgy entered the room almost simultaneously with her brief knock. "Rico is going to bring over the meal when it's ready. I thought Matt might like a few things from home. I called Ethel and she sent one of the boys in with some clothes and your toothbrush, some pajamas and a robe.''

''Pajamas? I wonder where she found those.'' Matt's gaze fell on Susan's heated cheeks, and he stumbled on. ''I, uh, I don't usually wear pajamas, that is, I—they must've been in my bottom drawer.''

Georgy chuckled. ''Most men don't bother with them, I've been told, so don't look so embarrassed, child. Now, do you want anything out of here right now?'' She indicated the suitcase setting beside her.

''A t-shirt and that robe would be nice.''

''Matt, I'm not sure you should move your arm that much to put on the t-shirt,'' Susan protested.

''Ah, it's concern for my arm that makes you say that?'' he teased, remembering her fascinated gaze when she looked at his chest. That look did more for his self-esteem than any compliment a woman had ever given him. He watched in enjoyment as her cheeks grew even hotter.

''Stop teasing Susan. As she said earlier, you sure don't show much appreciation for everyone taking care of you.'' Georgy sounded like his sternest teacher in grade school. But her words reminded him of something he had to say to her.

''Georgy, I'm sorry I embarrassed you earlier.''

''Doesn't matter. It was Sam you embarrassed. He's carrying a torch for Mary Lou. Can't even think of another woman taking her place. That's how some men are.''

''Why do you think that?'' Matt asked, watching her closely.

''I asked him once if a man ever got over his first love.'' She stared into space, her eyes filling with tears. ''He said . . . he said he guessed some men did, but he didn't think he ever would, even if he lived to be a hundred.''

''That idiot!''

''Matt! How could you say that?'' Susan demanded, putting her arms around Georgy again. Georgy stared at him, as if she couldn't believe his cruelty.

''Georgy, the man was talking about you!''

"Don't be silly," Georgy protested, her voice trembling. "He was talking about Mary Lou. She was his wife."

"The man just stood here in this room and told me he fell in love with you when you were sixteen. He said he married Mary Lou because *she* loved *him*. Not the other way around. He loves you and has since you were both teenagers. Now, what are you going to do about it?"

# Chapter Ten

Even Susan didn't speak as his aunt stared at Matt. To her, the three of them appeared to be frozen, like the mortals on *Bewitched,* the old television series.

Then, while she and Matt watched, Georgy's face took on a determined look that would have even given Hitler second thoughts and dashed out of the room.

"Georgy—" Matt called out as the door settled softly to.

"I think you're a little late," Susan advised him. "And if I ever have sensitive matters to be revealed to someone, I won't ask you to get involved."

"What are you complaining about? I just told her the truth. I was trying to help."

Susan drew an exasperated breath. "And you expect her to do something about Sam's stupidity? That's assuming that what you said was true. If it wasn't, your aunt is going to be horribly embarrassed."

Matt glared at her. "Of course it was true. And why shouldn't she do something about it? If a woman loves someone, then she ought to be willing to fight for him. It's not just a man's prerogative these days.''

Susan glared back. "Right. You men always embrace women's rights when it's something that benefits you."

His good hand suddenly became a fist, but he tried the same maneuver with his broken arm and groaned.

Immediately Susan was reminded of her role. She wasn't Matt's girlfriend, his lover, or even a friend. She was his doctor and it was time she behaved like one.

"I'm sorry. Please relax your arm," she ordered, her voice calm and impersonal, she hoped, as she placed her hand on his injured arm. "Take deep breaths," she added as his muscles were still bunched under her soothing fingers.

"I'm trying, damn it. Take your hands off me."

"Matt, I'm your doctor. I'm supposed to—"

"I don't care if you're the Surgeon General. I can't relax until you stop touching me. It makes me want to pull you into this bed with me and not let you up until Christmas." His voice was as tight as his muscles and he continued to glare at her.

Not very lover-like.

Susan stepped back from the bed and chewed on her bottom lip. "I didn't realize—"

"Yes, you did. You realized it when you removed my shirt. And don't lie. I saw it in your eyes." His voice softened. "I felt it in your kiss."

"*Your* kiss. I didn't start anything."

"You sure didn't stop anything, either." A look of male satisfaction was on his face and Susan wanted to hit him.

She sought the discipline that had gotten her through medical school when she'd thought she'd never get another good night's sleep. "I will in the future."

"Will what?"

"I'll stop anything in the future. We won't have—there won't be any more kisses to worry about."

She turned her back to open the curtains that covered the

one window in the room. Anything to give her time to compose herself.

"That would be a shame," Matt whispered. "They're the best damn kisses I've ever had."

Thrusting her hands into her slacks pockets so he wouldn't see them shaking, Susan kept her back to him. "Matt, I expect your cooperation. We've already discussed this—this aspect of our acquaintance, and we're both agreed that it should be ignored." Her calm words pleased her.

"I don't think that's what we agreed on." He was just as calm.

She turned around in surprise. "Yes, it was."

"No, it wasn't."

The man was intentionally being difficult. She remembered his wanting her to leave because, as he explained, she wasn't what he was looking for. "I'm a city girl, remember?"

"I remember."

"Then is our conversation coming back to you, now?"

"Lady, I haven't forgotten a single word you've said to me. And just because I don't intend to marry you doesn't mean I don't want you. Or enjoy touching you. And especially enjoy kissing you."

Color stung her cheeks and her breathing was growing shallow. In another minute he'd have her panting, she thought, trying to take deep breaths. The man could turn her on faster than a light switch. She'd never experienced such compelling desire before. Why?

Striving for a coldness to rival a deep freeze, she said, "And if you'll remember, I told you that wasn't enough for me."

"It sure felt enough in the examining room."

He was impossible. And he was right. For those few minutes, anything he offered her would have been enough. She had to get out of here.

"I'm going to check on your dinner." She didn't wait for an answer.

*   *   *

Damn! Was he crazy? Why would he make life difficult for himself like that?

Because he couldn't help himself. He wanted her in his arms again so badly he could taste it. He wanted to put his brand on her, keep her to himself.

But he couldn't marry her. Not that kind of brand. 'Cause she'd leave sooner or later. And he wasn't going to put himself through that pain again. It would be worse this time, much worse.

His pride had been damaged when Lindsay left. But his heart had scarcely been bruised. Even though he wouldn't admit it to anyone, he was kind of relieved when she left. His life had fallen back into a comfortable pattern. No longer was he living with a stranger who didn't want any of the same things he did.

And it would be the same with Susan, he assured himself. She wouldn't be interested in marriage, a family. She was a doctor.

But she didn't feel like a doctor in his arms.

Maybe he could coax her into having an affair while she was here. She wasn't going to stay, but they could enjoy themselves while she was the town's doctor.

Matt's lips relaxed into a smile as he imagined just how much enjoyment he would have if Susan agreed to his plan. He'd have to go slowly, of course, give her a chance to get used to the idea.

But he'd start right away. Maybe he could coax her into a goodnight kiss.

"Julio Franco is ready. The pitcher delivers. Wow! Look out, if it stays fair, it's outta here! Goodbye! Julio Franco has done it again! The Rangers lead, six to four."

The announcer's voice was excited, but Matt stared stonily at the screen. His idea of a cozy evening with Susan, the two of them watching the game together, hadn't materialized. He hadn't seen his dedicated doctor since he'd pushed her too far several hours ago.

His dreams and schemes had intrigued him for a while. Then he'd grown more and more irritable. The only diversion had been dinner, supervised by Rico.

Tonight, baseball couldn't hold his attention.

Much to his shame, while he'd imagined a warm and loving Susan, he'd even forgotten Sam and Georgy. After stirring that pot until it boiled, he should have at least worried about his aunt's happiness.

Instead of worrying about his satisfaction.

He drummed the fingers on his uninjured side on the mattress. He didn't have a phone in his room. He was a patient. He shouldn't be abandoned like this. What if something went wrong? He could fall out of bed or something.

Spotting the buzzer to call for help, he paused in his inner tirade. He shouldn't press that buzzer. After all, he wasn't injured. Only bored. Irritated. Damn it, where was she?

Without any more argument, he reached for the buzzer to summon help.

Within seconds, the door flew open and Susan stood there, looking at him.

"It really works." He tried to keep his words nonchalant even as his eyes devoured her.

"What's wrong?"

"I don't feel so good."

"Is your arm aching?"

She hadn't moved away from the door, and he wanted her closer. He tried to lift his arm off the pillow.

"Don't do that!" Susan admonished, rushing to his side.

He decided the pain was worth it as he breathed in her perfume. Her warm body pressed against the bed, just inches away from his fingers protruding from the temporary brace. Maybe he was losing his mind, but he felt alive again after two hours of simply existing.

"I'll get you—"

"No, I—"

"Matt? Susan?" Georgy's voice sang out down the hall.

Both of them turned toward the door. Matt was surprised when Susan gripped his shoulder. The tight squeeze told him how worried she was about what had happened earlier. But she wasn't any more worried than him.

"Georgy?" he called.

His aunt came through the door with Sam in tow. Georgy was beaming. Matt thought she looked almost like a teenager again, and he breathed a sigh of relief. Sam ducked his head as Matt's gaze traveled on to him.

"You were right," Georgy said, tears welling in her eyes again. She and Sam were holding hands, their fingers laced together.

Matt didn't respond to Georgy's words. He'd known he was right. But he hadn't been sure Sam would admit the truth. And he wasn't sure his good friend would forgive him for spilling the beans. "Sam?"

"Son, I—I want to ask for your aunt's hand in marriage." Sam's face was bright red and he was staring at his boot toes.

"I told him he didn't need to ask you anything. I'm old enough to know my own mind. The idiot doesn't think he's good enough for me." The blissful smile on her face told everyone Georgy didn't agree.

"Oh, Georgy, I'm so happy for you," Susan said, releasing Matt's shoulder and going to hug the other lady. Then she offered Sam a kiss on the cheek along with her congratulations.

Matt tensed again and then told himself not to be a fool. He couldn't be jealous of Sam. After all, the sheriff was marrying his aunt. But he wished Susan dared to come that close to him, to offer him such sweetness.

"When is the wedding going to be?" Susan asked.

"We haven't talked about that. We were too busy sorting

out our feelings. The fall would be nice," Georgy suggested, her gaze cutting to her intended, watching for his reaction.

"No, ma'am," he said firmly, straightening his shoulders, lifting his chin, once more the man in charge. "If you're crazy enough to marry me, sweetheart, it's gonna be right away. I've waited too many years for you as it is."

Georgy melted against him, her fair skin glowing, her delicate hands going to his weathered cheeks. "All right," she whispered, and his lips stopped anything else she might've said.

Matt averted his eyes, feeling like an intruder, but when his gaze fell on Susan, his need for her increased tenfold. Sam was a damn lucky man.

"Ahem!" he said. "You two are acting like teenagers. You could at least get in the backseat of a car."

Though both their faces were red, and they broke off their kiss, the lovers just stood staring at each other, silly grins on their faces.

"So when is this wedding going to be? I need to get my suit pressed so I can give the bride away."

"Law says we have to wait three days. I'm going to roust out the city clerk right now. It's only nine o'clock. Since today is Thursday, we can be married Sunday."

"Oh, Sam, should you do that?" Georgy asked. "We could wait until the next weekend if you don't want to bother Jack."

"It's no bother, Georgy darlin'. Sunday."

"Let's have it out at my place. We'll barbecue and invite the entire town," Matt suggested, his grin almost matching the other twos.

"Dadblast it, man, the whole town? The partyin' will never end," Sam complained, but the smile on his face negated his words.

"I can't think of anything I'd rather party about," Matt told him, wanting Sam to know how happy he was to welcome him into his family.

"You sure you have no objections?" Sam asked, a serious

look on his face. " 'Cause this is the only chance you're gonna get to stop it.''

Though Georgy protested his words, Matt ignored his aunt and stuck out his uninjured hand. "I'd agree to tomorrow if it was possible, Sam. Welcome to the family.''

Sam moved over to embrace him.

The emotional moment was broken up when Georgy stomped her foot. "Men!''

"Now Georgy, don't get all excited,'' Sam said.

"Maybe I won't marry you after all, Sam Dryson.'' She stared at him, her hands on her hips, anger in her eyes.

"What are you talkin' about? You already agreed,'' he roared. When she didn't relent, his face lost its anger and the sadness Matt had earlier witnessed came back. "Don't do this to me, Georgy. Don't play with my heart. I love you more than life itself. I couldn't bear it if—''

He couldn't continue because Georgy was back in his arms, kissing every inch of his face. "I didn't mean it, Sam. I love you. I'm going to marry you no matter what you say or do. As long as you love me.''

"Sweetheart—'' Sam tried to say, but then their lips met again and Matt and Susan were left to stare.

"Damn, but this is like going to a sexy movie. It should have an R rating, though, especially if they don't stop that soon,'' Matt told Susan, though his eyes were on the other two. He didn't dare look at Susan right now. He'd already noted a single tear stealing down her cheek.

"You just made me so mad acting like Matt's agreement was more important than mine. I didn't mean I wouldn't marry you,'' Georgy whispered fiercely.

"Honey, nothing matters more than you loving me. But me and Matt, we've been friends a long time. And you're a Griffin, you know, and—''

"She won't be after Sunday. I'll be the only Griffin in town,'' Matt teased.

"Then, son, I reckon you'd better get busy populating this

here town with some more Griffins,'' Sam teased back, contentment on his face as Georgy rested against him, wrapped in his arms.

Matt's gaze met Susan's and the longing that rose up in him was so powerful that he couldn't look away, couldn't speak. He could only stare at her.

''I—I'd better get Matt's medicine. It's time for him to take a pill. I'm so happy for the two of you,'' she added, patting Georgy on the back before she slipped from the room.

''You okay, son?'' Sam asked, looking concerned.

''Fine. I'm fine. Well, let's make a few plans for Sunday, shall we? We don't have much time to plan the best wedding this town's ever seen.''

Susan sat on a stool in the nurse's station, waiting for Sam and Georgy to leave. She didn't want to return and intrude upon their family happiness. And she didn't want the knife twisting in her heart.

She was so happy for them. And jealous. It was an ugly emotion. But she'd come to Griffin to find her family, happiness. Now she wanted more. She wanted—she wanted to be loved. The way Sam loved Georgy. And she loved him. It was in their eyes, their voices, their touch.

Total commitment. Not a roll in the hay. Not an affair. Not a marriage for social prestige and money. She knew, now, that even if her father accepted her, acknowledged her, she couldn't remain in Griffin. Because she was afraid she was coming to love Matt Griffin as much as Georgy loved Sam.

And he only wanted her.

''Susan? Is everything all right? You didn't come back,'' Georgy said as she peeked around the corner. Sam stood just behind her.

''I knew you had plans to make. I thought I'd wait until you were finished.''

Georgy gave an exaggerated sigh. "These two have gone hog wild. Will you be able to help with some of it?"

"Of course, Georgy. I'm only working in the morning. If the swelling on Matt's arm has gone down, I'll send him home, and I'll be at your service the rest of the day and Saturday and Sunday, too." She'd intended to go back to Dallas to pack more clothes and make some temporary arrangements, but that could wait another week.

"You're a dear. I'm glad you're here."

"It's amazing how fast you've settled in here," Sam said, smiling. "Doesn't seem like you've only been here a week."

"No, it doesn't, does it? You've made me feel welcome," Susan said, smiling, hoping the sudden tears would stay in her eyes and not run down her face.

"You take good care of Matt, now, and I'll see you tomorrow," Georgy whispered and tugged on Sam's hand to lead him away.

Georgy was a perceptive lady. Muttering a whispered thanks to her friend who'd spared her embarrassment, Susan wearily stood and picked up the small tray with the pill and a glass of water. Once Matt took his medication, she wouldn't have to worry about any more emotion this evening. They'd both get a good night's sleep.

"Where'd you go?" he asked as soon as she stepped into the room.

"I didn't want to intrude."

He grunted but didn't ask any more questions.

"It's time for you to go to sleep. Do you want a trip to the bathroom before you take this?" She tried to keep her voice calm and cool.

"What is *this*?" he demanded, a frown on his face. Susan could just imagine him as a little boy, resisting every effort to make things easy for him.

"It's medicine."

"For what?"

"For your broken arm."

"You mean they have a pill to fix broken bones? Why didn't you give it to me earlier?" His sarcasm tugged at her patience.

"Matt, this is a mild sedative to ensure that you get a good night's rest. Now, are you going to brush your teeth before you go to sleep?"

He gave her a hard stare and then ran his gaze down the length of her. The sheet was drawn up to the middle of his chest, and he wasn't wearing a shirt.

"You gonna stand there and watch?"

Susan was surprised at how much she wanted to answer yes. She was the doctor, not some woman out for cheap thrills. What was the matter with her?

"I'll be back in five minutes, if you're sure you can manage on your own."

"I'm sure. Leave the pill and I'll take it while I'm in there." He continued to stare at her.

She almost did as he asked. Then she remembered her early days in Pediatrics. Always watch the patient take the pill. Otherwise, a lot of good medicine went down the toilet.

"That's all right. I'd rather you wait and take it when you're in bed."

"Is it that strong?"

"No, of course not," she lied. "I just don't want to take any chances. Five minutes."

She spent those minutes trying to restore her professional detachment. As his doctor, she had no business thinking the thoughts he provoked, thoughts of touching, caressing, kissing. Their next meeting would be totally professional, she swore to herself.

When she came back, as promised, five minutes later, he was once again in his bed, the cover drawn to his broad chest. "Ready?" she asked cheerily, hoping to make their encounter brief.

"I really don't need that pill. I'm exhausted."

"But your arm will start throbbing, if it isn't already, Matt. As your doctor, I must insist you take it." He didn't look exhausted, except for the circles under his eyes. He looked ready to arm wrestle her over the stupid pill.

"No."

"Matt, please."

"I'll make you a deal," he suddenly said, a mischievous light appearing in his golden eyes.

Warily, Susan nodded. "What?"

"A goodnight kiss."

"What?" she repeated, stunned by his audacity.

"I'll take the pill if you give me a goodnight kiss."

"I think you watched Sam and Georgy too long," she retorted, frantically trying to think of some way to avoid his silly barter.

"Maybe. Just a kiss, Susan."

"That's not professional."

"Neither is not giving your patient his medicine." He grinned engagingly up at her, looking as innocent as a little boy with a frog in his pocket, planning a surprise for his teacher.

"Fine. Take your pill and I'll give you a goodnight kiss." She extended her arms so he could reach the tray while she stayed as far away as possible.

"Nope. The kiss first."

"Matt! I have agreed to your ridiculous offer. The least you can do as a gentleman is go first."

"Ladies are supposed to go first, but I guess I can concede the point tonight." He reached out and picked up the small cup with the pill. "You're sure you're gonna keep your promise?"

"I'm sure."

He swallowed the pill and drank half the glass of water, then lay back against his pillow, looking at her expectantly. "Well? It's your turn to make good."

Should she stall him until the pill started taking effect? At the most it would be only five minutes. But she had to keep her word. She ignored the anticipation that rose up in her. She was only kissing him to keep her word. Not because she wanted to touch him again.

Definitely not because of that.

She moved to the bed, lay her hands on his warm chest, her fingers sliding through those silky blond curls, and lowered her lips to his.

# Chapter Eleven

Susan made sure the nurse remained by her side the next morning when Matt's arm was put in a cast.

"That was a pretty strong pill you gave me last night," Matt said with a hint of accusation in his voice when she finally faced him.

"You needed your rest."

Kay, who attended high school with Matt, grinned. "You got Matt Griffin to take a sleeping pill? Why, he wouldn't take a pain pill when he broke his ankle playing football. Old Doc Brown tried everything to convince him. How did you do it?"

Susan had enjoyed the informality and friendliness of Griffin. But now she wished for the cold formality of the hospitals in Dallas where nurses would never ask personal questions. With her cheeks a flaming red, she continued preparing for the cast, saying nothing.

"She used psychology, Kay. She is one talented doctor."

The cocky grin on Matt's face irritated Susan. She'd like to embarrass him as he was embarrassing her, but she couldn't think of anything.

"Well, I can't wait to bring Billy, my little boy, to you for his shots, Doctor," Kay said. "It'll be a treat to see you use psychology on him."

"Sometimes children are harder to convince than adults," Susan said, "especially men."

Kay giggled and Matt gave her a challenging stare. She returned her attention to her work.

"Oh! I forgot. Matt, I heard this morning that Georgy and Sam are getting married. Is that right?" Kay asked, handing Susan what she needed before she could even ask.

"That's right."

"That is so wonderful. When's the wedding going to be?"

"Sunday afternoon at my place, five o'clock. Spread the word. The town's invited."

"You doing a side of beef?"

He nodded and Kay, matching Susan's requirements effortlessly, continued chatting about the wedding.

"Matt, I'm finished with your arm." Susan said with relief and stepped away to open a sack she'd left on the cabinet. "Kay, if you'll use this to make a sling for Matt, I think he'll be more comfortable." She held out a large blue bandana she'd purchased that morning. They'd also had a hot pink one, but she was sure Matt would have rebelled.

"Sure, Doctor. That'll make a fine sling," Kay agreed, taking the cloth from her.

With a sigh, Susan headed for the door, grateful to escape Matt's presence. She was a bundle of nerves, just being around him.

Denise's voice came through the intercom. "Kay, your husband is on line one. He says your youngest is upset and needs to talk to you at once."

Kay's face immediately reflected her concern. "Doctor, would you mind? I'll be right back."

With a feeling of inevitability, Susan smiled and agreed to Kay's departure, taking the bandana from her as she hurried out the door.

"Why do I get the feeling you were hoping to escape?" Matt asked her, a grin on his face.

"I don't know what you're talking about," she assured him, avoiding his gaze. She painstakingly folded the bandana into a triangle and then stepped to Matt's side.

"Shouldn't I put on my shirt first?" he asked, watching her.

She pressed her lips together in frustration. "Of course. Is it short sleeved?"

"Yeah. And probably as stiff as that cast. I can't convince Ethel not to use a pound of starch."

An emotion she recognized as jealousy surged through her with surprising strength. "Who's Ethel?" she asked as she walked over to the chair to pick up the yellow cotton shirt lying across it.

"My housekeeper. She's been with the family for more than thirty years."

"I see." She moved back to stand in front of him, watching his face. "So, you'll fire her when you marry that wonderful country girl you're looking for?"

"Fire Ethel? Hell, no! Why would I do that?"

"I just assumed you were marrying a country girl so she could cook and clean for you. Isn't that right?" She tried to hide her interest in his response.

"I'm not looking for a wife to make a drudge of her." He acted as if he resented her insinuation.

"Then why does she have to be a country girl? Do you plan on her riding the range, punching dogies?" She kept her eyes glued to the shirt as she unbuttoned it.

He snorted, ridiculing her question. "What do you know about punching dogies, or riding, for that matter?"

"I'll admit I don't know about herding cows, but I've done quite a bit of riding, English style."

"English style? You mean with one of those pancake saddles? Those are ridiculous."

"They require a great deal of skill from the rider, unlike

that big cradle you Westerners call a saddle.'' She looked down her nose at him, feeling quite superior.

"A cradle, huh? You try staying on a horse riding anywhere but in those tame corrals you call a show ring and you'll be grateful for a western saddle.''

"Perhaps.''

He shook his head in disgust. "Yeah. My wife will ride with a western saddle. And she'll wear jeans and a Stetson, not some English Derby get-up.''

"Oh. You intend to supervise your wife's wardrobe?'' She knew she should end this debate, tie up his arm and send him away. But somehow she couldn't do that.

"Lady, you're pushing me,'' he growled. "My wife will wear whatever she wants. Unless she's riding. Then she'll wear jeans.'' He drew a deep breath and leaned toward her. "And my wife will understand ranching. She'll want a big family, and she'll be there for me and my kids, whenever we need her.'' He was breathing rapidly when he finished.

She took a step back. Very softly she asked, "And when you're busy and don't need her? What will she do then? Stand in the closet until she's called? All you want is a robot with no needs of her own. If you find what you just described, you'll be miserable.''

"You don't know what you're talking about!'' he assured her angrily, sliding from the table.

"Yes, I do. No wonder your wife left you. You only took, instead of giving.''

"Damn you!'' he muttered and reached with his good arm to pull her to him. "Why do I let you get under my skin?''

Before she could answer, if, in fact, she could come up with a coherent thought, his lips covered hers. The energy from their argument only heightened the desire this man always aroused in her.

The shirt she'd been holding fell to the floor and her fingers traveled over his heated body, caressing, touching, memorizing him. She couldn't get close enough to him, though their bodies touched from head to toe. She wanted more.

He seemed to feel the same way as his good hand started unbuttoning the gray silk blouse she was wearing. She gasped for air as his lips left hers to follow his hands.

"Matt—"

Whether she'd intended to protest or encourage, neither of them would know, because his mouth returned to hers, bringing with it the daze of passion that removed reality.

"I'm back now, Doc—oops, sorry."

By the time they broke apart, Kay was already out the door, but the damage had been done.

Or perhaps, Susan thought as she moved to the farthest corner of the small room, breathing rapidly, smoothing down her clothes, she should consider Kay's intrusion as a rescue.

How could she lose her head every time the man touched her? Her husband had never inspired such interest. Or anyone else. She definitely wasn't a sex maniac. At least she never had been. Until she met Matt Griffin.

Matt took a step toward her and she lifted her hand to keep him away. She didn't trust herself any more than she trusted him.

"I was just going to—to repair the damage I did," he said huskily.

His gaze was focused on her chest and she look down to find her blouse gaping open. With a gasp, she turned her back to him and tried to put the buttons back in their holes. It was a struggle, her coordination having disappeared along with her good sense.

"Susan—"

"Take the bandana and your shirt and go find Kay. She'll tie it for you." She wished her voice had sounded steadier, instead of wavering.

He didn't say anything and Susan didn't know if he'd followed her order or was still waiting for her to turn around. Finally, footsteps moved across the room to the door.

Just before the door swung shut, he whispered, ''I'm sorry.''

So was she. Sorry she'd given in to the desire that had been building in her ever since he'd first touched her. Sorry that she'd found the one place she wanted to be when staying there was an impossibility. Sorry she'd fallen in love with Matt Griffin.

Her words hurt.

Matt thought about them for most of the day after he returned to the ranch. Did he really expect his wife to do all the giving? Had he treated Lindsay that way?

He was relieved when he convinced himself that wasn't true. At least, not with Lindsay. He'd tried to find mutual interests. He'd encouraged her to get involved in the community, to make friends. He'd even left his beloved ranch and traveled with her a couple of times.

No, he'd given to Lindsay. But she'd always wanted more. And she'd given nothing in return. Except sex. She'd seemed to think that was the price she had to pay for whatever she wanted. And sex with Lindsay didn't even compare to a kiss from Susan.

And that scared him.

He couldn't be in the same room with her without finding some way to touch her. His last thought in that hospital room last night was of making love to Susan. Understandable because at the time he was kissing her.

When he'd awakened this morning, he'd been smiling. But no Susan. He had no idea if she'd occupied the bed next to him during the night or not. He hadn't awakened, thanks to her innocent little pill.

When he'd finally seen her, Kay was with her. If it hadn't been for that phone call, Susan would've left him there with Kay, avoiding any personal contact.

The sun was setting as he thought again about those few

moments of holding her in his arms, their lips meeting, their bodies touching. Leaning against a corral fence, he found himself aroused just remembering.

It wasn't like she fought him. Hell, no! She met him halfway. As long as she didn't have time to think. He rubbed his face with a weary hand.

"You okay, boss?" Pony asked, putting one hand on the top rail.

Matt shrugged. "A little tired. Seems silly to let a broken bone take so much out of you."

"Maybe you need the doctor to make a housecall," Pony suggested, a sly grin on his face.

Matt groaned. "I see Kay's got the rumor mill going. You just forget whatever you heard, Pony."

"You mean you and the doctor weren't gettin' it on, like Kay said?" Pony asked, disappointment in his voice.

"I mean the doctor isn't our kind, and she'll be leaving real soon." That was the best answer he could give. He didn't want to flat out lie to Pony.

"I thought she was stayin' until you found another doctor."

"She is. But I'll find one soon. Real soon. So you just tell everyone to forget about me and the doctor. It won't happen."

"Whatever you say, boss. I'll tell the boys to quit wastin' their money bettin' on you strollin' down the aisle like Sam, giving up your single life." Pony walked away, laughing.

Somehow, Matt didn't think he'd convinced one of his best employees not to speculate on his personal life. He wasn't surprised. Hell, the whole town was probably discussing his chances of marrying the doctor.

They just didn't understand that marriage wasn't in the cards. Now, bedding the doctor, that was another thing. But marriage? He didn't want to marry the doctor, have a lot of little doctors, change diapers because she was too busy taking care of other people. He didn't want that.

Did he?

*   *   *

Susan pulled herself together and spent Friday afternoon with Georgy in San Angelo. When she'd returned to Georgy's after closing the clinic at noon, Georgy and Jenny had been waiting for her.

Though Jenny was Georgy's closest friend, they were both afraid her acting as Maid of Honor in the quickly assembled wedding would be too much for her. Georgy asked Susan to take her place.

She couldn't say no, so Susan threw herself into the planning of the wedding, hoping to forget her own broken heart. Gowns were of the utmost priority, and she and Georgy drove into San Angelo to buy gowns for the two of them and for Jenny since Susan forbade her to make the trip.

Saturday was spent organizing the honeymoon travel plans, helping Georgy pack, keeping her on schedule. The normally capable Georgy had become a basketcase. At any moment, she would drift off, thinking about Sam, and lose track of everything going on around her.

At least Susan had plenty to keep her busy.

But it didn't stop her from thinking of Matt.

Even worse, it seemed to her that everyone talked about the man. Georgy would reminisce about his childhood. Sam talked about how wonderful it was that Matt had brought he and Georgy together.

The friends who called on Georgy wanted to know Matt's opinion of the wedding. Of course, Susan came in for a few questions herself, and a lot of speculative looks. She should've known Kay wouldn't keep quiet.

Susan also regretted her cruel words to Matt. Who was she to cast stones? Her marriage hadn't exactly been a success either. But at least she knew what had gone wrong.

She'd been infatuated and pressured by her grandmother. He'd been looking for an easy ride. When he'd discovered her grandmother wasn't willing to turn over control of her fortune as she'd apparently hinted, he'd been ready to bail out.

With her grandmother's death, he'd changed his mind, but by that time, Susan's eyes were open.

She didn't think Matt was anything like Don, her first husband, but that didn't mean they were suited for each other. No. She was a doctor. He wanted a housewife. It just wouldn't work.

So she ignored any suggestive comments and concentrated on Georgy. At least to all appearances.

By the time she and Georgy arrived at Matt's ranch on Sunday, they were both bundles of nerves. Jenny was already there, and Susan met Ethel, Matt's housekeeper, for the first time.

"Welcome, Dr. Kelly," Ethel said, ushering her into Matt's home.

"Thank you. Please call me Susan."

"And call me Ethel."

Now that the amenities were out of the way, along with a certain sizing up of each other, Ethel relaxed and gave her a real smile.

"Well, you're not at all like that other one."

"I beg your pardon?" Susan looked around, seeing only Jenny and Georgy.

"Ethel, of course she isn't," Georgy protested.

"Well, I know you said so, but I had to be sure. I wouldn't want to live through something like that again."

"What are you talking about?" Susan demanded, her curiosity high.

"Matt's wife, that Lindsay. I was afraid, you bein' from the city and all, that you'd be like her."

"That seems to be a popular theory," Susan muttered. "I'm only temporary, you know," she hurriedly added, before any of them asked what she meant.

Ethel gave her a knowing grin. "Some folks don't think so."

Susan blushed a bright red and looked at Georgy for help. Since Georgy was grinning too, along with Jenny, she realized she was on her own. "Look, what—what everyone is talking about was just a kiss. And in this day and age, kisses don't mean that much. You know how men are," she struggled, not making a dent in those happy smiles.

"No. Why don't you explain how men are," a deep voice said just behind her.

She whirled around for her first look at Matt Griffin in three days. Unfair. He was dressed in navy blue slacks, a white shirt, its sleeve left unbuttoned over his cast, and a silk tie. The only part of his ensemble that gave him away as a rancher instead of a high-powered business man were his boots.

She closed her eyes to gather her composure, then looked him straight in the eye and said stiffly, "Hello, Matt. I didn't hear you come in."

"No, I guess you didn't. But I'm real interested in hearing what you have to say about men. You doctors seem to understand us men especially well, from what I've heard."

She knew he was referring to her accusations about his previous marriage. But she'd suffered enough the past few days, what with the staring and the difficult questions.

"I think I'll leave the explanation up to you, Mr. Griffin, since you're the one who caused the problem. Why don't you explain to these ladies why you were kissing me while I go powder my nose."

With a brief smile, she walked out of the kitchen, hopefully in the direction of a bathroom. Matt was left to face three very interested ladies. She wished him luck!

# Chapter Twelve

Matt stood in one corner of his almost completed hay barn, filled with those who attended his aunt's wedding. The ceremony had taken place outdoors, with his mother's flower garden as a backdrop.

Now he searched the crowd for a dark-haired beauty who was causing him all kinds of trouble. Susan's exit line in his own kitchen had only been the beginning.

"Well, Matt, are you going to explain what Kay saw?" Georgy had asked when he'd hesitated in his response.

"Nope. I don't think I will." He quickly changed the subject before Georgy could protest. "Sam sent me in here to see if you'd changed your mind. He still can't seem to believe you're willing to marry him."

Those words had distracted Georgy, as he'd intended. But the crowd was buzzing about the supposed romance between him and Susan, and he'd received numerous looks and teasing remarks about the two of them.

Then his nemesis had appeared in a rose silk dress that hugged her curves and destroyed his concentration. Big puffed sleeves emphasized her pale shoulders, and they always seemed to be in danger of slipping down her arms, leaving a man breathless with anticipation.

When his gaze finally located his quarry, he was irritated to find her in Pony's arms, dancing around the large barn floor. The role of host had kept Matt from joining in the dancing until now. He didn't want anyone else dancing with her, even though he knew he was being unreasonable.

The song was coming to an end and he pushed his way through the crowd.

"That was some fancy boot scootin', Pony," Matt said, congratulating his friend.

"Thanks, boss. But this little lady makes me look good." Pony beamed, perspiration rolling down his round face.

"Good. I'll borrow her for the next dance and see if I can learn a few steps." Matt didn't wait for Susan's assent. He was afraid she'd refuse. Slipping his good arm around her slim waist, he pulled her close as a new song began.

"I don't recall your asking me to dance," she protested stiffly, even though she was following his lead.

"I didn't." He couldn't say much else. Her closeness was affecting his breathing. The song was a romantic ballad that allowed him to hold her close, and he was satisfied.

She didn't make another protest or pull away. In fact, they seemed in sync as they moved around the floor. It was a rare occurrence, he decided, until he remembered the other times he'd held her in his arms.

He pulled her closer, eliminating any daylight between their bodies, even managing to maneuver his cast around her. The silk beneath his fingers slid against her smooth skin. Her soft breasts pressed into his chest. Matt danced toward the shadowed door at one end. When the dance ended, he'd need to stay away from the bright lights for a while.

Her hair was a wild tumble of curls below a confection of roses on top. He buried his nose in its silky depths, breathing in the combination of shampoo and perfume and Susan. "I've always wanted to touch your hair," he murmured.

She drew her head back and looked at him, an unreadable expression in her eyes. Then, without comment, she returned her cheek to his jaw and raised both arms to encircle his neck.

When the song began winding down, Matt discovered a powerful reluctance to release her. Without much consideration, he danced through the barn doors out into the almost-dark night. Susan's head, resting against him, came up when they escaped the brightness of the barn.

"What are you doing?" she asked breathlessly, her blue eyes wide.

"Just dancin'," he assured her, before his lips covered hers, turning his response into a lie. He couldn't have resisted the urge to kiss her, touch her, for a million acres of Texas land. She was too much temptation.

Her mouth opened to his and he deepened the kiss, pressing her body ever closer. She could never be too close. He wanted to touch every inch of her, to kiss her soft skin, to caress her.

The hand on his injured arm buried itself in her long silken curls, sensually weaving its fingers in and out. He broke off the kiss to stroke her neck and those tempting shoulders before returning to her swollen lips, slanting his mouth across hers, drinking deeply of her sweetness.

Her hands slipped beneath his arms and around his body, stroking his back through his shirt. He burned to peel off his clothes, to offer himself to her touch. She seemed as eager to deepen their embrace as him.

"Doc? Susan?"

A loud voice intruded on their sensual moment. Matt tried to ignore the voice he vaguely recognized as Sam's, but he felt Susan withdrawing.

"Anyone seen the doctor?" Sam called again.

"I—I have to go," she whispered, and he felt a shudder of withdrawal rack her body, making him only want to press her closer.

"Ignore him. He'll give up," Matt whispered, his lips searching hers once more.

"No, he needs me." She pushed against his chest.

"*I* need you!" He refused to let her go, frustration fueling his anger.

She shoved away from him with more strength than he'd expected as she called, "Sam? I'm out here."

By the time she reached the doorway of the barn, Sam had arrived. Matt stood back in the shadows, his gaze detailing her mussed hair, her swollen lips, her trembling body.

"There's been a major accident on the highway other side of Griffin. Lots of injuries. Will you come?" Sam had hold of her arm.

"No!" Matt protested, stepping forward. "It's your wedding day, Sam. Let your deputies handle it." He didn't say it, but he didn't want Susan leaving either.

Sam gave him a hard stare. "They're young, Matt, and sounded really shaken. Apparently, it's a bad scene. I've got to go. Georgy understands."

"My bag's in Georgy's car," Susan inserted, tugging on Sam's arm. "Let's go."

Matt stood there in frozen silence, watching them leave. He hadn't even realized Georgy had come to stand beside him until she spoke.

"It's a shame. I'd better go cancel those plane reservations we made. Looks like we won't be leaving tonight."

"Sam should've let his men handle the accident. It's not fair to you, Georgy." He wanted to protest something, but he wasn't sure what. Susan had to go. She was a doctor. That was why he wouldn't marry her, wasn't it?

His body still hadn't settled after the abrupt cessation of desire. He gripped Georgy's shoulder as much for himself as for her. "It's still a damned shame."

Georgy smiled up at him. "It's not so bad. I waited a long time for Sam Dryson to come to his senses. The important thing is that he'll be back. I know he'll always want to come home to me, wherever he is.''

"And that's enough?" He studied his aunt's serene smile.

"That's enough."

He had a lot to think about.

Georgy went to the house and changed clothes. The seriousness of the accident had a sobering effect on the guests, and most took their leave. A three car pile-up was a rare occurrence in or around Griffin. There were reportedly numerous injuries. Both nurses had left with Susan and Sam.

Matt left Pony in charge of the party and strode to the house. He met Georgy just coming out. She was dressed in slacks and a matching knit shirt.

"Where are you going?" he asked, noting the car keys in her hand.

"I thought I'd go back to the house and see if Maria and Rico were willing to go to the clinic with me. The three of us can do mop up duty. I'm sure they can use extra hands." Her employees had left the wedding earlier.

Matt nodded. He could understand Georgy's desire to follow Sam. He felt an urgency to be at Susan's side. "I'm going to change and I'll be right behind you. Even with a broken arm, I may be able to help."

She gave him a warm smile, patted his shoulder, and hurried away.


Susan had done a tour of Emergency Room duty, so she was prepared for the horrible sight. Even so, she felt as if someone had kicked her in the gut.

The two deputies had extricated six bodies from the cars. Susan and the two nurses immediately started triage, determining those with the greatest needs. Two teenagers, their bodies reeking of alcohol, were unconscious. One of the deputies had applied a rough bandage to stop the bleeding on an arm wound. Susan left those to Kay and moved on.

One man was dead. She shook her head and turned to discover a small child, curled into the fetal position. Blood covered her face, but Susan discovered no head wounds. She assumed the blood came from someone else. But the child was in shock and suffering from internal injuries.

Susan grabbed a blanket Sam had in his vehicle and covered the child. After checking the other two, a woman and another child, probably thirteen or fourteen, and telling Leslie what to do for them, she returned to the smallest patient.

"Sam?" she called, unwilling to leave the little girl's side.

"Yeah?" he called back, trying to extricate another person from the last car.

"I need to get this child to the clinic."

"Take my car. I can't leave."

Susan didn't argue. Lifting the small, still form, she struggled over to Sam's car and placed her on the back seat. Then she returned to the nurses.

"I'm going to have to operate. Can one of you come with me?"

Leslie said, "Kay, I'll stay here. You help Susan. You've had more training in surgery than me."

The two women hurried to the car. Susan slid behind the wheel, started the engine and had them moving as Kay snapped her safety belt.

"How do you turn on the siren?" she asked tersely, her eyes on the road.

Kay leaned over and pushed the button that activated the siren and the flashing lights.

"There's no ambulance here?"

"No. The mortician in the next town has one that we can schedule if we have a patient to move. But we've never had an accident like this one before."

Kay looked as shocked as Susan felt. In less than a quarter of an hour, she'd gone from Matt's intoxicating kisses to the stark reality of the accident.

And in the back seat, a small child was depending on her expertise for her very life.

They were surprised to discover the lights on at the clinic when they reached it. Rico immediately appeared at the door and came to carry the child inside.

"Thank you for being here, Rico. Is Maria—"

"She and Miss Georgy are inside," he assured her.

With Georgy and the others to handle any details, Susan and Kay immediately prepared the child for surgery and then, leaving Georgy beside the little girl, she and Kay scrubbed for surgery.

Matt arrived at the clinic just after Susan had gone in to scrub up. When Georgy came out and told him they hadn't yet brought in the other victims, he headed back to his farm truck.

He'd thrown in a big tarpaulin across the bed of the truck. He figured it would be easier for transporting people than a car. It took only a couple of minutes to reach the accident. The carnage was worse than he'd ever seen. He had never gotten sick at the sight of blood, but he'd never faced this kind of scene.

"Matt. Thanks for coming. Can we use your truck?"

"Of course, Sam. That's why I brought it. What can I do to help?"

"We just got the last one out, but he's dead. Let's get those who are alive back to the clinic. Leslie?" Sam called to the nurse tending the injured.

"Yes, Sam?"

"Can they be moved?"

"Yes, but be real careful."

Sam directed his two deputies to come help lift the victims into the truck. Though his broken arm frustrated him, Matt managed to help. All five injured were loaded onto the flat bed of Matt's truck.

"I'll ride back here," Leslie said, scrunching down in a small corner.

Matt circled the truck to slide behind the wheel.

"Wait, Matt, I'm comin' with you," Sam called before he turned back to give directions to his deputies about covering the two dead bodies and clearing the highway.

Soon they were on their way back into Griffin.

"Georgy's at the clinic," Matt said tersely.

Sam frowned and said, "Look, Matt, I know you're angry that I messed up our wedding, but—"

"No, Sam. I know you had to go. And Georgy understands. That—that was a terrible accident. How did Susan . . ." He trailed off, unsure what he was asking, wishing he'd been with her, wanting to know if she'd been strong.

"Susan did fine. She didn't waste a second on hysterics or tears or anything. She went right to work. Probably saved several of those people back there. Leslie and Kay were terrific, too."

It struck Matt that he had little interest in Leslie and Kay's experiences, even though they were both lifelong friends. He was only interested in Susan.

He eased the pickup into the parking space in front of the clinic. Rico joined them as they got out of the car, and the three men and Leslie began carrying in the injured.

With Kay in surgery with Susan, Leslie dealt with the injuries as best she could, and the others assisted in cleaning up the patients. Sam collected the personal effects of each person as they were undressed, marking down identification as he found it.

When all the patients were taken care of, he began the painful notification of family where he could. Pony and another of Matt's employees turned up with some sandwiches made from leftovers at the wedding, and Maria filled the large coffee pot in the waiting room. Still Susan and Kay were in surgery.

Matt finally looked at the clock and discovered it was one

in the morning, over five hours after Sam had interrupted him and Susan at the wedding.

Georgy slipped into the Waiting Room and walked over to touch Sam's shoulder as he talked on the phone. He reached out to slip an arm around her waist and pull her against him, even as he continued to talk.

"Matt? There's little else to do if you want to go on home," Georgy whispered.

He only shook his head. It would be impossible to leave until he saw Susan, knew she was all right. "How are things going?" he whispered back, motioning with his head beyond the Waiting Room door.

Georgy shrugged, a weary look on her face. "It shouldn't be much longer, according to Leslie."

Sam hung up the phone. "That's the last one, I think. I'm not sure about the child Susan's with, but she probably belongs to one of those people in there."

"Are they coming here tonight?" Matt asked.

"Yeah. Some should be arriving any time. One of the teenagers lives north of here about twenty miles. The other one was from Ozona," he said, naming a town about forty miles away. "The family was traveling. They're from Fort Worth."

"Was the father one of the deaths?" Matt asked.

"Yeah. It appears so. And one of the men in the third car. His buddy survived. At least so far."

"Will you have to stay?" Georgy asked.

"Someone's got to be here when these folks arrive, Georgy, darlin'. Do you mind?"

"No, of course not. I'm going to send Maria and Rico home. But first I'll pour you a cup of coffee. Matt, you want some, or are you leaving?"

"No, I have to—I'll wait with Sam." He couldn't explain the need to see Susan, to be sure she was all right. After all, he had no legal or moral right to stand beside her. But he didn't really have a choice. He wasn't going anywhere.

"I need to call Ethel. She'll be up, worrying about me," he suddenly remembered.

"Why don't you use the phone in Susan's office," Sam suggested. "I have a couple of more calls to make to get things squared away."

With a nod, Matt went into Susan's office. He came to an abrupt halt. There, on the floor, was the rose silk dress Susan had worn in Georgy's wedding. He picked it up, somehow expecting it to be warm and vibrant as it had appeared with Susan in it. Instead the material was cold, unwelcoming. As he turned it over, he discovered the front of it smeared with drying blood.

He laid it across the chair beside the desk, then reached for the phone. After talking to a relieved Ethel, he hung up the phone and stood there, unsure what to do.

The door opened and he spun around to discover Susan leaning against the wall just inside the room.

"The operation's over?" A dumb question, he reminded himself.

"Yes." Her voice was a whisper, exhaustion lacing it.

"You need to get off your feet," he said, hurrying to her side. "How about some coffee, a sandwich?"

She avoided his gaze and shook her head.

"Susan? Are you all right?"

Slowly, she raised her face and he looked into her tragic eyes for the first time. "I'm all right. But—but I couldn't save *her.*" Her voice ended on a sob that brought Matt's good arm around her.

She buried her face in his shirt and quietly cried.

# Chapter Thirteen

It took several days to clear up all the difficulties created by the wreck. Susan felt like an intern once more, working with little sleep and more to do than was humanly possible.

Sam and Georgy got away for an abbreviated honeymoon Tuesday evening. The last of the patients was dismissed then also. The two more serious injuries had been flown back to Fort Worth.

"Kay?" Susan called as she left her office Wednesday just before noon.

The nurse stuck her head out of the last examining room they had used. "Yes, Doctor?"

"I think that's the last patient."

"It was. And I told Denise not to let anyone else in unless it was a real emergency."

"Good." She smiled at the nurse. "I just want to tell you how well you did these past few days. You and Leslie were wonderful."

Kay smiled but shook her head. "It was a real pleasure to

watch you operate, Doctor. I can see why you're not staying in Griffin.''

Susan looked away. "That's not the reason. I'd—I'd love to stay here, but some things just don't work out the way we plan them. Anyway, I need to go back to Dallas for a couple of days to take care of a few things. Pack some more clothes. I've asked Denise to reschedule everything for next week. If you or Leslie could be on call for emergencies, I'd appreciate it.'' She needed a break from the emotional roller coaster she'd been riding.

"Sure. You are coming back, aren't you?'' The edgy look on Kay's face brought a smile to Susan.

"Yes, I am. But Griffin existed without a doctor for several years, you know.''

"Yeah, but I like it better when you're here.''

They exchanged smiles and Susan returned to her office to put things in place before she walked to Georgy's and packed a bag.

Kay hurried to a phone.

Susan had already contacted Curtis about flying her to Dallas, but he was unavailable. Instead, she'd begged a ride to San Angelo from one of Sam's deputies. From there she'd take a commercial flight to Dallas.

She came down the stairs at Georgy's with her bag, setting it in the hallway and stepping into the kitchen to tell Maria and Rico goodbye. When she came back out to wait for her ride, she discovered Matt, dressed in jeans and a knit shirt, his Stetson pushed back on his head, waiting.

"Matt. What are you doing here?''

"Heard you needed a ride to San Angelo.''

She hadn't seen him since Sunday night. She'd been embarrassed that she'd broken down and cried all over him. Since he hadn't come near her since then, she could only assume he'd been disgusted. Looking over his shoulder, she hoped the deputy would arrive. "I've made arrangements, but thank you anyway.''

"He's not coming, Susan."

Her gaze whipped back to his face. "Why?"

"I told him I'd take care of you. Sam only has three deputies. You might endanger the entire population of Griffin if you took one out of commission to drive all the way to San Angelo."

"I—I see." With a shrug, she reached for her bag. "I appreciate your driving me, then."

He took her bag from her with his good arm. "You'll have to get the door, if you don't mind. Did you tell Maria you were leaving?"

"Yes."

Instead of his Jeep Cherokee, he led Susan to a gleaming Cadillac Allante. Its sleek silver-blue exterior contrasted beautifully with the white leather interior.

"Nice car," she said, frowning. "Is it yours?"

"Yes. I keep it for special occasions or long drives."

As soon as he'd put her suitcase in the back seat, he slid behind the wheel and cranked the engine. Immediately a burst of cold air blew on Susan's hot cheeks.

They drove for almost a quarter of an hour without speaking. Finally, Matt asked, "When are you coming back?"

"I'm not sure."

She felt his gaze but she continued to stare at the road in front of them.

"You are coming back, aren't you?" he asked sharply.

"Yes. I told you I would remain until you found another doctor." She waited for him to say something but he didn't. "Have you found any prospects?"

"No."

His brief answer was the last word spoken for several miles. Then he said, "I heard from Sam and Georgy just before I left the ranch. They'd reached Denver."

"Oh, good. I'm sorry they were delayed."

"Couldn't be helped." He cleared his throat. "The town was really impressed with your work Sunday night."

Susan gnawed on her bottom lip but said nothing.

Matt looked over at her before returning his gaze to the road. "Kay said you're an excellent surgeon."

She looked out the side window.

"Susan, you can't blame yourself for that child dying," he said softly.

Blinking her eyes quickly to dispell the moisture that gathered there, she said, "I know. But it still hurts when a small child— it's hard to take."

"You did everything you could."

"Yeah."

"Georgy told me about some of the programs you want to start. I'll help you with any of them."

"Thank you." She stole a look at his handsome profile, wondering at his change in attitude. He seemed to accept her as the doctor of his town now, temporarily. At least he wasn't shoving the temporary part down her throat anymore.

He also wasn't treating her like a woman he wanted in his bed. Had he finally lost his desire for her? She stared straight ahead, that thought making her sad. Maybe, having seen her as a doctor, he no longer thought of her as a woman.

She wished she could make that transition as easily. But Matt Griffin was still the most desirable man she'd ever met. When the time came to leave Griffin, her heart would break.

"Why are you going back to Dallas?" he asked abruptly.

"I have some things to take care of. I was only planning on a brief visit when I left."

"I guess your friends were surprised when you didn't return." He looked at her out of the corner of his eyes.

"Yes."

"Any special friends?"

She frowned at him, a question in her eyes.

Sighing, he said, "I'm trying to ask if you're involved with anyone."

"You mean a man?"

"Who else would you be involved with?"

She swung her gaze back to the road. "No."

She didn't understand why he was asking that question now. The idea had never occurred to him when he was pulling her into an embrace, kissing her as she'd never been kissed before.

Just thinking about those kisses sent a shiver down her spine. She snuck a look at him as he drove one-handedly.

"What about your ex-husband? Is he in Dallas?"

"Yes."

"Do you ever see him?" His knuckles were almost white as he gripped the wheel tightly.

"No."

"What went wrong?"

She turned to stare at him. "Why do you want to know?"

He shot her a look she couldn't interpret before he returned his gaze to the road. "I've told you about my marriage. You've even analyzed it yourself. It only seems fair that you tell me about yours."

She didn't want to talk about her marriage, but, somehow, she couldn't refuse. "It was a mistake. Other than marrying me for my money, he also didn't want someone with a career. Sound familiar?"

He frowned. "But didn't he know you were a doctor?"

"I wasn't then. We married when I finished college. He agreed I could go on to medical school, but both he and my grandmother thought I'd get pregnant and give it up."

"But you didn't."

She shook her head and added wearily, "I'm a doctor, Matt. It doesn't mean I'm not a woman. It doesn't mean I don't want children. But I will always be a doctor."

He didn't respond to her words, and she fought to keep her expression impassive even though she felt like crying.

"I'm still a little tired. If you don't mind, I think I'll nap until we get to San Angelo."

"Go ahead. You've earned a little rest."

She didn't intend to go to sleep, just avoid making conversation with Matt. But the long hours she'd worked caught up with her and the next thing she knew, Matt was waking her. He'd parked the car at the airport and was opening his door.

"Oh. I didn't mean to—there's no need for you to get out. I can manage from here. You've got a long drive back."

He ignored her protests, retrieved her bag from the back seat and stood waiting for her to join him.

"Really, Matt," she started again as soon as she reached his side. The heat rose up from the concrete, a contrast to the cold air inside the car.

"Come on," he muttered and strode toward the terminal.

If she wasn't going to be separated from her bag, she was going to have to run. He might have a broken arm, but his long legs were in perfect working order.

"Matt, I can't keep up. You're going too fast," she panted, feeling moisture beading on her forehead.

He abruptly slowed down, turning his head to wait for her. "Sorry."

Maybe he was in a hurry to be rid of her. Her thoughts were growing gloomier and gloomier. Was it because she didn't want to leave Griffin, or Griffin's mayor? She didn't want to answer that question.

They checked her bag and then Matt escorted her to her gate. Boarding hadn't begun, but she turned and stuck out her hand. "Thanks for driving me. That was very thoughtful of you."

"Take a seat," he said, gesturing to the plastic seats beside the gate.

"There's no need for you to stay, Matt."

He ignored her again, removing his Stetson and sitting down, stretching out his long legs.

Susan finally sat down beside him, unsure what she should do. Since he had nothing to say, she remained silent also. Finally, the stewardess announced her flight. She and Matt stood up at the same time, and again she extended her hand.

Before she could begin her prepared speech of thanks, he said, "I never shake hands at airports. It's bad luck."

"Oh!" Susan said, blinking in surprise. "I didn't know that."

"That's right. No handshakes. Only kisses." Without waiting for her agreement, he pulled her to him, his lips taking hers. For one brief moment, Susan rediscovered the magic his touch always brought her.

He lifted his mouth and whispered in her ear, "Hurry back." Then he released her and walked away, his long legs covering the distance quickly.

Susan stared after him until the hostess tapped her on the shoulder. Following her into the plane, Susan could only believe that Matt still thought of her as a woman, a desirable woman. She didn't think he'd ever kissed a doctor like that before.

Matt drove the highway to Griffin by memory, his mind on the woman he'd just left.

Kay's call at noon surprised him. He hadn't realized Susan would leave today. He'd stayed informed of her hard work through Georgy. When his aunt left last night, she'd told him Susan would need a few days to recover from the stress and work she'd been through.

He agreed to give her a little space, though he was impatient to see her now that he'd done some thinking. The discovery that he was in love with Susan Kelly had come as a shock. But when he'd held her in his arms after her patient had died, he'd known.

He hadn't wanted to be anywhere but with Susan at that moment. Not because he would be satisfied sexually. Not because he would have fun. Not because she would cook him meals, or have his children, or any of those other reasons he'd been using.

He wanted to be there because she needed him.

It was as simple as that.

And the thought of not being there when she needed him, or not having her beside him when he suffered, was unbearable.

It was a powerful emotion, love. What he'd felt for Lindsay had been a combination of lust and infatuation. He wanted Susan, more than he'd ever wanted a woman. But he wanted so much more.

He'd wandered about the ranch, his mind grappling with how much he needed her, how little his rigid plans for the future mattered. Ethel had prodded him from one chore to another with cheerful patience. Once, when he'd snapped out of his thoughts, she'd teased him about another wedding in the future. He hoped so.

But he'd never discussed a future with Susan. He'd discussed sex. He had no doubts about their mutual attraction. But would she consider marriage to him? Would she believe his change of heart? That he wasn't trying to control her or deny her her career?

After what she'd told him about her first marriage, he could understand reluctance on her part. But he couldn't think of trying to keep her from being a doctor after he'd seen her commitment, her courage, her . . . heart. So he'd dealt with a rewrite of his future, with Susan by his side, until the idea seemed to have always been with him. And he was waiting until the right moment to inform her.

Then she'd left town.

What if she didn't come back? He'd go get her, he immediately decided. If nothing else, they had the physical attraction to build on. He'd convince her to at least give him a chance.

And when she got back, he'd go to Fred. It wasn't fair to Susan to expect her to live in his town and not be recognized as Fred's daughter.

He wanted to make everything right for her.

Because he loved her.


Susan wandered down the massive staircase in her grandmother's house. Her house now, actually, but she had difficulty thinking of it in those terms. When she'd left Dallas two weeks ago to interview in Griffin, she'd been undecided about the future of the house.

Now, she knew she'd never live in it again.

There were too many bad memories. Good ones, too, but even if she came back to Dallas to live, she'd want to start over. With a decided nod, she hurried her steps and went to the phone at the bottom of the stairs.

In only a few minutes, she'd contacted a friend who worked in real estate and set up a meeting. A feeling of relief filled her, telling her she'd made the right decision.

Her life wasn't here. More and more, she realized she wanted to put down roots in Griffin. With Matt. She wrapped her arms around herself and remembered his touch with longing.

She shook off her imagining and strove to think more practically. With the money she'd get from the sale of the house, it suddenly occurred to her that she could help her father's home town. There'd be money for sonogram equipment, a neo-natal unit, and even an ambulance.

It seemed fitting to her that her grandmother should pay to improve the lives of the people she'd scorned, in particular her father. He was being given a second chance at parenthood, and she was being given a chance to make amends for her grandmother's wrongs.

The next few days were incredibly busy. And lonely. As she went about her tasks, her thoughts invariably turned to Matt. Did they have a chance for a future together? As she conducted an unending debate, she worked, sorting out the household items she wanted to keep and having them moved to storage. When she set up house and started her own practice, she would use the familiar things again.

The rest of the household would be sold in an estate sale. The Mercedes she'd driven was traded in for a Ford Explorer, practical for the roads around Griffin and for transporting patients.

Sunday afternoon, after visiting a friend while the agent

showed her house, she returned home to an excited message on her machine. Her agent had a buyer for the house.

Susan signed the contracts that evening. She'd have to return in about six weeks to close on the house, but other than that, she'd settled her life in Dallas.

Monday morning, she loaded the Explorer bright and early and set out on the long drive to Griffin, Texas.

She felt like she was going home. To Matt.

All she had to do was convince him that a life together was possible, even if she was the town doctor.

Her heart ached with fear that he'd reject such an idea. But at least she could go back and try to convince him. For now, she was their doctor.

She could go home to Matt and Griffin, Texas.

Temporarily.

And only hope for more.

# Chapter Fourteen

Susan didn't reach Griffin until Tuesday morning. An unexpected blow-out caused by a piece of metal that flew off a trailer in front of her had delayed her trip. She'd decided to stay in a motel in the small town a couple of hours from Griffin, rather than drive in late Monday night.

After all, she hadn't told them exactly when she'd be back.

Since her car was new, no one realized the doctor had returned until she reached the clinic. It was already nine-thirty. She would go to Georgy's to unpack later.

Sliding out of the Explorer, she stretched her legs. Then she reached back inside for her purse and medical bag.

"Hey, Doc, welcome back!" someone called from across the street. Susan waved, happy to be back. The town looked so different than her first view of it.

Opening the door of the clinic, she greeted Denise with a smile.

"You came back!" the teenager exclaimed. Without waiting for Susan's startled response, she ran to the connecting door, opened it and called, "She came back!"

Kay immediately appeared beside Denise, and they stared at her as if neither could believe her appearance.

"What's the matter? I said I'd be back."

Kay hurried across the room to hug her. "I know, but when you didn't come back Sunday night, everyone decided you had second thoughts."

Susan laughed. "No. I was anxious to get back, but I had a lot to do. Do I have any patients this morning?"

"Not really," Kay said, ushering her into her office. "Jenny Slater is due in to have her blood pressure taken, but I can do that if you want to go on over to Georgy's. The honeymooners are back, and as happy as can be. It just does your heart good to see them," Kay assured her with a big grin.

Susan listened to Kay's update on the gossip of Griffin as she cleared her desk of letters and papers that needed her signature. She enjoyed catching up on the lives of the citizens of Griffin.

Denise stepped to the door. "The Slaters are here."

"Want me to take care of Jenny?" Kay asked.

"I'll do it. I want to keep a close eye on her. Would you mind filing these papers for me?"

Denise had shown the Slaters to the first examining room and Susan entered just as they were sitting down.

"Susan! You're back!" Jenny exclaimed, jumping up and hugging her.

"Of course I'm back. I can't believe it's such a surprise to everyone." She even grinned at her father over Jenny's shoulder.

"We're glad to see you," Fred said, his gaze warm and friendly.

"Thanks," Susan murmured as she stared at him. Then she cleared her throat and pulled Jenny back so she could look at her. "And how is my patient? Are you taking those naps, like I said?"

"Every day. Fred insists," Jenny said with a roguish smile at her husband. "And he hired a very nice lady to come in at noon each day. She fixes our lunch, cleans house, and cooks dinner before she leaves.''

''Perfect. Sit on the examining table and I'll take your blood pressure.'' Jenny complied with her directions and Susan then asked her to lie down. Already, at three months, Jenny was beginning to show the growth of the baby.

Afterwards, Susan moved over to make notations on the chart and Fred joined her.

''Is she doing all right?'' he whispered.

''She's fine. Everything's progressing as it should.''

''How strange,'' Jenny said, and they both turned to look at her.

''What, Jenny? Is something wrong?'' Susan asked, seeing nothing to explain her patient's remark.

''You and Fred.''

Susan looked at her father and saw the alarm in his eyes. She turned back to Jenny, trying to keep her face blank. ''Yes?''

''You have the same eyes and eyebrows.'' Jenny cocked her head sideways, still staring at the two of them. ''Come to think of it, you even have his nose, Susan, only yours is a little smaller, more feminine.''

''Maybe our ancestors came from the same cave,'' Susan commented lightly and turned back to her chart.

''She looks like me because she's my daughter,'' Fred blurted out, looking at first Jenny and then Susan.

Susan put down the chart and moved to Jenny's side. ''Take deep breaths, Jenny, and remain calm.''

''I'm not shocked, Susan,'' Jenny said calmly. ''I've suspected since the beginning.''

''What?'' Fred roared. ''What are you talking about?''

Jenny smiled serenely. ''Susan looked at lot like you. Then I remembered you said your daughter's name was Susan. She was about the right age. I just couldn't figure out why neither one of you was admitting it. I thought maybe you didn't know, Fred.''

Fred stared at his wife, confusion on his face. Susan took

Jenny's hand. "He didn't know at first, Jenny. When I told him, he didn't want you to know because—because he was afraid you'd be upset."

"Why?" Though Jenny asked Susan, her gaze was on her husband.

"We'd just had that talk a few weeks before, Jen, when you got upset that we'd never have a child. I didn't want Susan's being here to make you feel bad."

Jenny's eyes filled with tears and she reached for her husband. Susan moved back so the two could embrace, but Jenny, from her husband's arms, spoke to her. "You probably don't realize what a sacrifice that was for Fred, Susan. He used to talk about you, worry about you, a lot. He kept a picture of you in his desk drawer."

"I didn't know you knew about the picture," Fred said, searching her face for any pain.

"I knew," she whispered, cupping her husband's cheek with her hand.

"Jenny, I wanted to meet my father and—and explain to him about not answering his letters, but I don't have to have public acknowledgment. I want you to be happy, and I want my little brother or sister to be healthy." Susan avoided looking at either of them.

With a chuckle that warmed Susan's heart, Jenny said, "I'd prefer that we shout it from the rooftops. And this baby will be thrilled to have you for a sister. In fact, I'd count on a lot of free babysitting if you were going to stay—surely that's not the reason you refused to stay?" Jenny demanded, sounding upset for the first time.

She must've read the guilty look Fred and Susan exchanged.

"Why, Fred Slater!" Jenny exclaimed. "I can't believe you'd let Griffin go without a doctor just because—"

"He loves you more than anything in the world?" Susan reminded her. "I think maybe he deserves a hug instead of a chewing out, Jenny."

"Maybe," Jenny grudgingly admitted, but she linked her

hands behind his neck. "Anyway, now you can stay, Susan. You can be our permanent doctor."

Susan stared at her, unsure how to respond.

"Don't you want to stay?"

Susan stared at the two of them, people she'd come to love in their own right, not just because he was her father. Yes, she wanted to stay. A month ago, to be welcomed into her family would have been enough to make her ecstatic. But now she needed more.

"Yes, I want to stay, but—but there are complications."

"You mean, more than me?" Fred asked, surprised.

"Of course more than you, silly," Jenny said, hugging him close. She smiled at Susan. "You mean Matt, don't you?"

Susan nodded.

"How'd you know that?" Fred demanded.

"I saw them dancing at the wedding. They were looking at each other the way we did, the way Sam's been looking at Georgy and vice versa." Jenny looked Susan in the eye. "What are you going to do about it?"

Her words were a challenge quite similar to the one Matt had given Georgy. Susan remembered Matt's statement that a woman had as much right to fight for her happiness as a man did. He was right.

She leaned forward to kiss first Jenny's cheek and then her father's. "I'm going to go have a chat with Matt Griffin," she said firmly.

"Good for you!" Jenny cheered.

Susan didn't have much time to prepare her speech, since Matt's ranch was so close to town. But she was determined about one thing. She was going to be Griffin's doctor.

Staying here would give her time to convince Matt that she could be his wife and the town doctor, too, if he loved her. She was afraid it would take a lot of convincing. But she had one thing on her side. He wanted her.

At least it was a start.

She parked her new Explorer behind his Jeep and hurried over to the back door. No one used front doors in Griffin.

Ethel must've seen her coming because she opened the door before Susan reached it.

"You came back!"

"Yes. I said I would."

"We were all worried. Of course, not as much as him," she said, motioning behind her with her head.

Susan peered around her but couldn't see anyone. "Matt? Is he here?"

"Sure is. He's in his office, just down the hall, second door on the right. Go on in. He'll be really pleased to see you."

As Susan walked past her, she added, "And the rest of us will be pleased, too. He's been a bear."

Susan could only hope Ethel meant he'd missed her. She'd certainly missed him. The door to his office was standing open and she could hear his voice. She stepped inside the room, but his back was turned to her and he was speaking on the phone.

"Yes, Dr. Hulsey, that's right. It's a wonderful town, and a doctor is needed . . . yes, the package does include that . . . the interview will be a mere formality. Your past record has already convinced them . . . Next Monday. Perfect. I'll look forward to meeting you."

Susan stood there, pain almost making her fall to her knees. In all her plans and hopes, she'd never considered that Matt might find another doctor to replace her.

He knew another doctor would mean she had to leave. Her temporary stay would be over.

She fought the tears that filled her eyes. He didn't even want her in Griffin temporarily anymore. He didn't want her at all. She turned to go. There was nothing left to say.

"Susan!" He was out of his chair, around the desk, and beside her before she could persuade her body to move. "Thank God you're back," he added, and gave her a one arm hug.

His warmth enveloped her, and she longed to raise her lips

to his, to show how much she'd missed him, but she couldn't. She had to hold herself rigid, or the pain she was feeling inside would rip her apart.

"Yes, I'm back."

He leaned away from her, a puzzled frown on his face.

"You don't sound very happy about it."

"I gather I need to pack my things."

"What? What are you talking about?"

Anger was forcing its way in among the pain. "You were talking to a Doctor Hulsey?"

"Yeah," he agreed in a distracted manner, running his good hand up and down her arm. "He wants to get out of the rat race."

"I'll leave in the morning," she said, her voice leaden.

His hand closed around her arm. "What are you talking about? You can't leave. I've worked everything out. I want us to have a chance, Susan, together. We can do it!"

The anguish in his voice almost matched her own, but Susan knew he was wrong. If Griffin had a doctor, there was no place for her to practice. And if Matt Griffin had so little respect for her career, then he didn't love her.

He didn't love her.

She could no longer hold in her anger and pain.

"I'm a doctor, Matt!" she yelled. "I can't be anything else. I *won't* be anything else. If you—"

His lips covered hers, but Susan fought him, shoving against his solid chest, turning her lips away, though they were dying for his touch. She needed him so badly, but she couldn't give up herself, who she was.

Neither of them would be happy if she did that.

"Sweetheart, of course you're a doctor. You're Griffin's doctor."

Susan grew very still, hoping she hadn't imagined his words. "What?"

"I said," he repeated patiently, a warm grin on his face. "*You* are Griffin's doctor."

This time she accepted his kiss, but she couldn't enjoy it as much as she usually did. "Then what were you telling Dr. Hulsey?"

Matt grinned. "I was telling him about the opening for a doctor at Big Lake, about twenty-five miles from here." He smoothed back a strand of hair that had escaped her braid. "I think things will work out well. He'll be close enough that you two can give each other a weekend free, vacation time, even a short maternity leave."

A burgeoning happiness was filling Susan, but she wanted confirmation. Leaning against his muscled body, she asked softly, "Why would I need a maternity leave?"

Even his broken arm, cast and all, went around her as he cuddled her against him. "Because I can't live without you."

Her arms slid up his shoulders to link behind his neck. "But you understand about my being a doctor? I can't always be here."

"I know. But I'd rather have what I can with you than with anyone else in the world. I love you. I love the part that's a doctor as much as the part that's the sexiest woman in the world." His kiss this time was much more satisfying to Susan.

It was almost too much. She'd thought she'd have to convince him about their future and he had it all planned.

"You haven't said you love me," he reminded her.

"You think I kiss all my patients the way I kiss you?" she asked, her eyebrows soaring.

"You'd better not. Those kisses are all mine."

"Yes," she agreed simply, pressing against him. "You're sure Big Lake wants this doctor?"

"Oh, they want him. Their clinic isn't finished yet, and they still have to find some more financing, but when I contacted them, they were so excited they started planning all kinds of activities to raise money."

"I think I know where they could get matching funds," Susan said slowly, her head resting on Matt's shoulders.

"Where?"

"I sold my grandmother's house. I wanted to use the money to help Griffin, so I bought a lot of equipment and a new ambulance."

"Must've been a big house," he muttered as he nibbled on her neck, sending delightful shivers down her back.

"Mmmhmm, but there's lots of money left over."

"Sweetheart, you don't have to use your own money to finance the new doctor."

Susan wasn't sure he was concentrating on her words since his good hand was unbuttoning her blouse.

"Damn, how much longer does this cast have to stay on?" he demanded in frustration.

"Four more weeks. The new doctor would help me, as you pointed out."

"Mmmhmm," he agreed, his lips trailing the opening in her blouse.

"In case I need a maternity leave."

She'd gotten his attention.

"You do want kids, don't you?" he asked anxiously as he raised his head. "I can cook, and I'll help with the diapers, but I can't have 'em without you."

"Yes, I want your children, Matt," she whispered. "Maybe we can convince Ethel to help with them."

"I know we can," he assured her with a grin. "And I'll talk to Fred. Now that Jenny's—"

"We've already got that settled. Our children will have grandparents."

Matt grinned down at her. "Well then, doctor, the only thing left to do is to treat your patient."

"And what patient is that?" she asked.

"Me. I've suffered waiting for you to come back to me."

"I'd never turn away a patient," she whispered, her lips seeking his. Her hand left his shoulder to close the door. It was time for a private consultation.